Unalienable Rights

From the Melvin Time Chronicles

By

Mark Wayne Allen

<u>Other Writings by Mark Wayne Allen</u>

AWARDS AND PUBLICATIONS

<u>Awards</u>
First place poem Parish Fair - Life, The Miracle
Fourth Place (Writer's Conference)

<u>Books</u>
Star Siege
3 Lifetimes In 1
Force Of Life - From The Melvin Time Chronicles
Introspection - From The Melvin Time Chronicles

<u>Publications</u>
Dementia e-zine - This Land Is Your Land
Dementia e-zine - Johnny
Dementia e-zine - Discovery

Bayou Writers Group Anthology Vol. 2
Bayou Writers Group Anthology Vol. 1
15 Articles in "The Voice of Southwest Louisiana"

Cover artistry by Mark Wayne Allen.

www.markwayneallen.com

From the author

There was a long period in my life when I thought this novel would never be completed. To tell you why, I have to take you back to when I was 12. I suffered a major burn over 42% of my body. My mother and I lived as one person until I was back in school. At the age of 15 the pressures from the burn and a hematoma that altered chemical balances in the brain led to an attempted suicide. After that I became a quadriplegic and my mother lived our lives as one person yet again.

When I say one person, I mean she was caretaker, emotional support, psychological therapist, friend, companion, driver, and all else. She was all that and much more for about the first 30-something years of my life. When she died, it left a crater in my life. This novel was about 30% done at that time. Her death crushed me. I did not do anything constructive or forward living for a long time, although my wife may disagree. I tried many times to advance this novel, but the farthest I could get would be a couple of words or a sentence and this was 15 months post-funeral.

My wife was so patient, it is beyond words, and I thank her for that. This carried on for years. Eventually, I added whole chapters.

WOW! Everything was progressing, but agonizingly slow and I was still nowhere near the end.

You never expect the cataclysmic. Translation: Our house was struck by 2 hurricanes and a tornado head on. My wife and I have been evacuated for almost a year.

I've been asked many times how to write a book. This novel is the epitome of that advice because after those disasters, I, literally, had to pick up the pieces and move on. I kept writing words, sentences, paragraphs, or whatever came to mind about my ideas. One scene leads to another, such as, if I come home from work tired of problems, I might talk to my wife a while, eat dinner, and then lie down. The actions are all progressive. They all build on each other.

It took a lot of chain writing like that to finalize this book. It might not have taken this long yet had it not been for the hurricanes, tornadoes, and other events that were beyond anyone's control. They killed our home. Fortunately, in-laws took us in and after I got beyond the immediate problems, with other major problem setting in, I became depressed and lethargic, apoplectic even, but I kept on pushing.

If it hadn't been for some great people, this book might still be in limbo.

Introspection (book 1 of this series) started out without sequels, or a series, in mind. When I got finished with it, I discovered a wrinkle that never really got answered. I, and others, thought that the content and quality of the book merited another book.

I must say that I'm happy with the way it turned out. I hope you are too.

This book is dedicated to Wayne and Judy Koehler for their steadfast help in the aftermath of Hurricane Laura and to all people that try recover from tragedies.

1

Melvin woke to a gloved, sweat-soaked hand smashing his lips into the teeth beyond. Blood spewed into his mouth from busted lips. It was repulsive... He swallowed hard as his fists knotted up. Yick! He strained to breathe through pinched nostrils. The odor was the stench of humanity, in its full glory, and it was assaulting him, burying his face deep into a pillow.

He could feel hands clutching his wrists and ankles, pawing at them in disrespect. The tearing of duct tape pierced the room. It was the rebuke of an activity or lack of and in his experience as a private eye, familiar. This was different though. Margie was here! Damn them! He felt the pressure of his arms and legs being thrashed about and tightly wrapped.

What in the hell was going on???

He struggled against the bonds, to no avail. Damn it! He thrashed about while more blood spewed down his throat. Whoever this was had rendered his muscular frame helpless.

Bumping noises to his right made his head turn. Hollow-rage ran threw him at the sight of more black figures doing the same to Margie. Damn them! He thrashed about in fright for his lover and the bitterness of his soul which she helped calm. The heathens also put giant rows of duct tape over her eyes and cheeks. As they wrapped her arms and legs, one person stuffed some kind of white cloth into her mouth.

Bastards!

The figure in front of him put his hand on the right side of Melvin's face blocking his view and the muscled arm started forcing his head away. Melvin struggled against the movement, but when another black figure to his left grabbed his head from both sides, the force became too strong. He could struggle and bounce, but his head was going to move. As it did, he cut his eyes and glared at the garbed figure towering above him. Struggling to mutter unkind words while he thrashed about, he saw that the shadowed eyes in the dark bedroom did not waver or even blink.

"Listen here you asshole...."

What was that accent? Australian, British, African? Definitely a high-pitched male....."

"We know Tom Soren brought you some stuff and we damn well want it! You can either bring the stuff to us today ten a.m., the same Wal-Mart you usually shop at, or this girl bloody well dies! You understand me, Yank?!?"

Melvin blurted a muffled, "Fuck you!" as best he could. Tom Soren has been dead for three weeks! This mess was supposed to be solved!

"To make sure you do your best, we'll be taking your girl with us. You'll both be fine as long as you do what you're told. If not, we'll let your girl have us 'real' men, then we'll kill her. Bet you'd enjoy watching that, huh? After that, we'll teach you some lessons until we get our answers and then maybe feed you to the ants. Not so quick that way.... More enjoyable....

Just so's you won't forget, we typed a card for ya. Show him the card." The black figure beside him held up a small paper about the size of a business card, then bent down and laid it on the bed. "Okay, Fellas, let's go."

A black figure went out of the bedroom door with a squirmy dark sack thrown over his right shoulder. There were muffled cries coming from within. He'd kill 'em if they hurt her! He flounced about but soon realized he was not going anywhere and finally laid his head back onto the pillow.

As soon as everyone but two figures exited the room, the one at the foot of the queen-sized bed pulled a gun from his right side and said, "Don't move, Buddy. I would hate for you to loose a shoulder. We're just going to go."

Another brit accent or something....

The figure in the front said, "Alright, Cracker, get us what we want and you'll both live. Don't dare move until we're out of here." The hand pulled away from Melvin's mouth. Watching the pistol in the other man's hand, Melvin didn't move. He didn't dare....

Melvin glared at the figure that had released his mouth and was backing away. He considered cursing at the black figures as they moved toward the door, but didn't. Maybe he could get set free of his bonds. "How do you expect me to do anything bound up like this?!?"

"You're a resourceful chap, you'll figure out something."

"Geez! What a kind-hearted person you are!!!!!"

The figures were almost beyond the bedroom door when the main guy reached over and grabbed the knob. As he pulled, he said, "Yeah, I suppose you're right. ... I'll just close this here door and give you some privacy." Kloomp!

Melvin's body trembled. He could shout, but what was the use. As he lay with everything but Willie exposed, he heard the front door slam shut.

2

Melvin slammed his eyelids shut and squeezed them hard. He could feel the storm of his miserable position settle upon him. Lord, let it be a dream, he wished in silence. Shaking his head on the pillow, he could feel his gut tell him otherwise. The salty taste of blood was streaming over his tongue to his throat, forcing him to swallow the icky stuff, and he could feel his hands still bound in front of him.

"It's a nightmare! It's a nightmare!"

He shook his head before daring to open his eyes again. When he did, his vision was slightly fuzzy. He stared at the brown speckles on the white ceiling and decided to fixate on one larger speckle in the shape of a football until his vision cleared, then turned his head to the right.

All he saw was the dingy blue sheet, brown blanket, and white comforter mussed up and misshapen. Damn! Closing his eyes once more, he rolled his head back.

"Chester, I need a break," he said, remembering his old bartender on Kay Street. Clark had always been a good at listening to his troubles, unfortunately, this was simply a continuation of his human existence.

He raised his arms in front of him. Yep! Still taped together. Seeing was believing. Melvin pulled them apart as hard as he could. Grunt... grunt... grunt! Moaning and whaling, he pulled his arms. He could see the tape stretching slightly with each of his attempts, but still holding firm. He made a few more attempts before gasping for air.

He dropped his arms with the hands nearly nailing his groin.

"Careful, Melvin," he muttered. He laid his head back on the pillow and gulped a few breaths of the cool morning air. It was mid-February now, the roughest winter season for the Baton Rouge area. Although the mighty Mississippi river never froze, a lot of the small creeks in the area did, just like his life. The passage of time had warmed up for an all too short of a time with Margie, but now his life lay there in a frozen quagmire again. Disgusting!

Just when he thought his life was about to get better... he should've known that something would have to happen. Rekindling his love for Margie years after their divorce was certainly something he never counted on. He had his only friend in a rotten world to thank for that. A month ago, Tom had reappeared after twenty-years, dropped a bombshell in his lap, then died. If it weren't for that, he would have never called Margie for help.

Who would ever have believed that you could point a ray gun at someone and reverse their cells back in time, make them an infant, or even wipe out their conception??? It was crazy! If Tom hadn't shown him that dead roach and de-aged it, bringing it back to life, he would have never believed it.

Well, he couldn't waste time pondering the past and mulling over how good or bad things were. He picked his arms up, pulled and grunted, but dropped them again after stretching his restraints a little more, but this time being more careful of Willie's jewels.

Footsteps across the pine decking outside aroused him. What now, he thought, as he heard the metal-layered front door crash open. Muffled voices and footsteps made him wary of his intruders. Lying on the soft bed, he could feel the vibrations of footsteps searching for Lord knows what. Here he was, helpless, with nothing covering his groin but bed linens. He was certain that he could free himself given time, but it was the one thing that he didn't have much of. Bound up like a cow, moving anywhere would make too damn much noise.

He looked to his right at the jumbled bedding and began trying to free his arms again. After only a few moments, he found that the muscles were tiring. Drat! Not wanting to make any extra noise, Melvin relaxed his prone position and stared at the hollow-paneled bedroom door. It was tissue paper between himself and invaders, but it was all he had.

The many heavy footsteps inside the house reminded him of the beatings of the African drums in a Tarzan movie. The gold doorknob was turning. Oh crap! Now what?!? All he could do was sit back and take it like a man. Life had given him the big green wiener weeks ago and now was thrusting.

The door glided open and Melvin saw a figure slowly enter the room. The tall man's pitted face was unmistakable. It was Mike! When he saw Melvin lying there restrained by layers of gray duct tape, he looked over his shoulder and shouted with a deep voice, "In here!" He looked back at Melvin and squinted. His black suit made a slight ruffle as he snapped a salute and smiled. "Quick, quack, Melvin. Remember me?"

3

"Mike Curry, you son of a bitch! Get me outta here!" There was no time to think or waste. His love was being carted off to God knows where and he was determined to get her back safe. Rocking back and forth, he tried to stretch his arms again. "Come on, Man! Don't just stand there! Help me!"

Mike reached for Melvin's wrists and started unwinding the gray tape. "Melvin, you have no idea what's happened in the past three weeks." He balled a sticky wad of tape in his hands and then threw it toward the floor. It stuck to his hand as he released it so he rubbed the mangled mess on the side of the bed and then reached up to grab more.

A wide-eyed Melvin could only manage to stare. What's going on?!? What pieces of the puzzle were missing?!? As he curled up into a sitting position, his legs still on the bed, three more people entered the bedroom: a dark haired man, one older with a graying fringe, and a brunette. They began freeing his legs.

Although fury was in his heart, Melvin simply said, "I'm surprised to see you, Mike, but in my present situation, very glad," Melvin said. The lying corners of his mouth tugged upwards as Mike reached for the remaining tape on the hands. "Please forgive me, but... why are you here? What's happened in the last three weeks?"

Mike's pitted face stared a moment, then said, "I hope you'll understand this, but we've been monitoring your house."

"What in the world were you thinking, Mike??? *That's an invasion of privacy*! A big one!!!"

Mike freed Melvin's hands and tossed the remaining tape in his hands onto the floor. This time the mass was sent flying into a corner. Melvin tried moving his legs, but saw the three others still trying to unwind the tape.

Mike looked at the gray-haired man a moment, then turned back toward Melvin. "The justice department started a background investigation on time reversion technology. Top Secret! In the first few days, one of the investigators was witnessed to be getting younger and younger until finally he simply was not there anymore. No one even remembers him except the man that saw him disappear."

Melvin's legs were free now and he pushed his hands to the mattress swinging his legs over the side of the bed. The horrible blood taste from his lips had made him nauseous. Putting a hand over his mouth, he reached for the paisley-blue tissue box on the nightstand, grabbed one the white papers, and put it to his mouth.

Tilting his head back, Melvin put both hands behind him and propped on them. With his right hand, he palmed the card that the Brit left. He saw Mike squinted and surveyed the position, but Melvin didn't think he noticed the card.

"There's a much better way to treat that mouth," the graying man said.

"What's that?"

He stepped into the bathroom, came back with a tube, and squeezed out a blob onto two of Melvin's fingers. "That's tootphaste. Rub it on the inside of your lips. It'll stop the bleeding and make it heal quicker. ... By the way, I'm not sure you remember me, but I'm Roger and this Judy Green."

Before he knew it, Melvin had huffed and grumbled, "I remember you." He regretted perhaps insulting one of his rescuers, but Roger was the one who had locked him, Rob, and Margie into that accursed limo without telling them and this Judy wasn't even there. Perhaps if Rob hadn't tried to be so sly, he would've been calmer.

The memory of past treachery created doubts in his mind. Squinting, he glanced toward the floor. When he looked up, he gazed into Mike's eyes. He could feel calm return as he asked, "If nobody else remembers this guy, how did you get involved?

"I happened to talk to the guy that saw all this later that day. We were both involved in the investigation into Senator Gold's involvement. He mentioned to me what he had seen and, knowing the situation, I decided to covertly start investigating the matter.

Because of the disappearance, I knew that there must be at least one more, if not several, other organizations conducting research into time reversion. I talked to the NSA director and, after a long conversation, my team was put in charge of the investigation. I was assured complete autonomy with full military and intelligence resources. I report directly to the NSA assistant director, Charles Maywear, with presidential oversight. The justice departments records were sealed, of course.

The reason we were keeping an eye on you is we suspected that they might return to you."

Melvin stared into Mike's eyes for a moment. It was absurd to think that such strange news as this could be anything other than the truth. No matter how crazy it was, it would be just like crazy humans to steal, pervert, and abuse anything that would give them any power or money. Idiots! What insanity!

He looked down a moment and made tight fists with his hands and saw his knuckles turn white and the fingernails bury deep into his flesh. The pains allowed him to focus and then look up at Mike. He dare not react too emotional. "I love Margie! She is my only concern."

"I understand that, Melvin. We want to get her back too."

There it was again. The familiar rush of blood, undoubtedly flushing his face, was unmistakable and Melvin could feel beads of sweat on his forehead. "The material that they want is destroyed!" He put a hand to his face and wiped. When he withdrew his hand, he looked down at the drenched skin.

"Are you okay?"

Sitting back onto the bed, Melvin sad, "Yeah, but Margie and I burned all that stuff up in a fire the night this all ended! ...At least, I thought it ended...." Melvin stomped his right foot several times in rage at himself. How could he have been so short-sighted. "Damn It!""

Going through hell once was bad enough, but coming back willingly for a second

dose of the same thing was horribly wrong.
What will a man go through for love? How far
will he go? How long? Question after question
kept popping into his mind. He heart was
telling him that his love was limitless, but his
mind was filled with questions about the nature
of human flaws.

Yes, he loved Margie, but limitless?
Everybody was flawed. Everybody will
disappoint.

Mike took a step closer. He lowered his
head a bit, then immediately raised it. He
lowered his brow and said in hushed voice,
"I'm sorry to have to ask you this, but would
you please work with us to get this horrible
technology stopped?"

There it was. It was a call for help. They
needed him. Now, this was a situation which
he liked. Mind, be damned, his heart knew
Margie would remain true and, damn it, if she
could, he could. Besides, he was holding Mike's
key to get into the game. "Yes, I'll help you, but
I want your assurance that we'll do everything
possible to keep Margie alive? She means much
more to me than you could ever realize?"

Mike glanced downward. When he
looked up again, Melvin saw his brown eyes
turn black for an instant. He felt his guts quiver

for a moment. Was it his imagination or did it really happen?

"We'll try our best, 'Melvin. That's the only thing that I can guarantee."

"I guess that'll have to do." Melvin looked down at the gold Timex that Margie had given him a week ago while they were shopping at Wal-Mart. "Six a.m.! We've got to get moving!"

4

"Hello. This is Margie. I don't know where I am because I can't see anything. My eyes are covered with tape or something. Of course I'm bound up, but I hear the road noise of a traveling vehicle. I think I'm in the trunk because I hear the whirring of wheels on the road and the axles buzzing about. It's cool in here too.

Since I won't be doing anything productive for some time, I wanted to take this opportunity to tell you a bit about Melvin. I know he can be difficult to deal with. He is a loner that likes to be completely self-reliant. I had to wait twelve long years to convince him that I was faithful in my love for him. That is how pig-headed he is. Until recently, he was convinced that he was infallible with perfect understanding of himself, others, the world, and all else. His decisions and opinions were always the correct ones.

I finally managed to show him that his problems with humanity, men and women, were at least partly within himself. I convinced him to trust in me for a start. That sounds like a very small step, but let me assure you, it's not. His stubbornness to not realize the complete understanding of anything doesn't only come from himself, is unequaled. With his realization of my love, I hope, that's starting to change. It's not much, but at least it's a beginning.

I hope he can free himself to trust others more. He is going to need help at some time in his life, just as I need help right now. I have faith that he will come."

*

It was 8 A.M. before Melvin finished talking with Mike and left the house. He agreed with the game plan that they had devised although his gut rumblings were telling him that something was amiss. He didn't trust them or anyone else, but, for the moment a least, he needed some kind of a plan and as bad a plan as Mike had devised, it was all he had.

He told Melvin of a contingency plan that his FBI team had used in the past of having a wreck on the way to the drop off point. It would supposedly allay suspicion and give them time to gather intelligence. Mike said that it was rare for the victim to be put in danger this way. Melvin couldn't help but laugh in his face. It wasn't the best thing he could've done, yet it happened, and he couldn't take it back. He didn't want to apologize, but he did to not piss off the only help he had. A poor plan was better than no plan. Right now, they had no information about anything and needed time to get it.

He didn't necessarily trust Mike or anyone to get it either.

During these past three weeks he had gained a trusting relationship with Margie, but as far as anyone else... Ha! This was the first time he had trusted anyone since his younger days with Tom, a good friend that ended up deserting him after high school and again after dropping a bombshell in his lap. Melvin's heart was not like that. He had given it to Margie and would kill anyone to save her! He knew her like he knew himself. She was his priority, his heart, and God help anyone who got in his way.

He gripped the gray-plastic steering wheel of the Ford Pinto that the FBI had loaned him going South on Airline highway and was supposedly going to be in an auto accident at the corner of Bluebonnet. Supposedly injured, they would take him to Our Lady of the Lake Hospital, put him in isolation, then figure out a better plan.

He supposed all the local news networks and papers would be blanketed with the story. Those people that had Margie would investigate his supposed demise before doing anything else. Melvin didn't want to gamble with Margie's life. It made his gut ache.

This was completely different than poker though. One particular item kept scratching his brain though.... How did anyone know that Tom gave him anything? Only he, Tom, and the people of Earth, Inc., who were all supposed to be in prison, knew that. Was it just supposition on somebody's part... or, did they really know for sure?

He was in the left hand lane doing 35-miles-per-hour and approaching the intersection with Old Hammond Highway when the white pickup in front of him slammed on its brakes. Melvin saw it plenty of time and began to swerve into the right lane, but saw that a white Jeep had pulled alongside him. His quickly placed a foot on the brake and mashed down hard. His torso pitched forward even though both hands gripped the steering wheel with stiffened elbows. When the dinky car completely stopped, his torso flung backward and then lurching forward, his forearm immediately went to his gut. "Damn!" There was the old feeling again! His insides quivered as he propped against the steering wheel. If anything happened to Margie....

The car door beside him clicked open. Melvin leaned back and looked at the rugged face.

"Easy, Mac, just come with us," a masked, gruff voice said.

Melvin' balled up a fist and swung at the guy, but discovered hot sweaty arms entangled with his and were draging him out of the car.

"Okay, Bruno, knock him out."

Melvin felt a sharp stick in his left arm and then everything went black.

5

At the Mall Of Louisiana, Mike and two others were sitting in a black sedan trying to watch for the people that Melvin was supposed to meet. The parking lot was filled with every type of vehicle imaginable and it was bumper to bumper with almost every slot filled. It was Saturday and everyone and their pet lizard were enjoying the mall.

The sky was filled with stratus clouds which hindered visibility. They weren't rain clouds, just annoying when searching for details. The morning weather report on 102.5 FM indicated that today's high was supposed to be forty-six degrees. That was a balmy day in Wyoming, where Mike was born, but with the Louisiana humidity, it was chilly, to say the least. Wyoming's dry cold didn't it seep into your bones as much. Louisiana, on the other hand, is always wet and cold weather is like diving into a pool of ice water.

The watery areas in the parking lot left over from last nights rain were probably near freezing. Mike gazed at the puddles until a passing car woke him from his dreamy state He scanned the overcast skies and for the helicopter that would never come. They could have used one to make observations, but that would have instantly alerted whoever it was that, 'Hey, you're being spied on.' Mike could not allow that to happen. That could potentially risk everything and those were contrary to his orders. They would just have to make do with a ground view.

The radio strapped to Mike's waist squawked and a voice said, "Team one to team two."

Mike grabbed the device from his belt. "Team two here. Go ahead, Roger."

"Melvin should have been here ten minutes ago and the GPS tracker shows that he has been stopped for at least fifteen minutes. What shall we do?"

Mike depressed the button on the side of the walkie talkie. "Just give him a little more time. He knows the plan. .... Wait! Where did his car stop at?"

"Airline and Old Hammond."

"That area is known for traffic accidents. It would answer the reason for the delay." Mike looked down at his watch. "It's 9:41 right now. Hold your position and we'll try to track his path."

"Roger, Team Two."

Mike grimaced as he clipped the phone to his waist. He reached for the car key, grabbed, and turned. The sedan's engine revved up as he said, "Keep your eyes peeled. I have no idea what's going on, but we can't just sit here." He looked to his right. "What do you think, Sam?"

Sam turned toward Mike with an open-mouth. His squinchy eyes stared a moment. With a lick of his lips, the mouth closed, swallowed. He looked over his left shoulder and stared at Peter. "I don't know about you, Dude, but I think this is way too important to just wait.

Peter looked at Sam for a second, stiffened his lips, and then looked at Mike. "As much as I hate leaving our position here, I agree. We can't be too careful with this. We are under orders, after all."

Mike looked at them both. "Then we're off."

*

The entire trip took only a few minutes. When they arrived, Mike saw three police cars, their blue lights flashing, in front the Ford Pinto. Two officers, with traditional city cop blue uniforms, were on the driver's side of the car with notebooks and pens out talking to a few people, writing as they listened. The driver's door of the Pinto was open and the car was vacant. "Uh-oh," Mike whispered to himself seeing neither Melvin nor wreck. A third officer walked up, took a handkerchief out of his pocket, wrapped it in his hand, and closed the Pinto's door by pressing a few inches underneath the door handle. The fourth man was observing one of the conversations, occasionally nodding, but incessantly writing on a tablet.

Mike turned left as soon as he could and parked near the Hammond Air Plaza. The three men opened the doors of the sedan and walked over. Mike reached into his left jacket pocket, grabbed his I.D. and brought it into the sunlight.

"Mike Curry, FBI."

The officer looked up from his writing and said, "Yes, Sir, how may I help you?"

"Do you know where the driver of this vehicle is?"

"No, Sir, nobody does." He pointed to himself. "By the way, I'm Chris Green. According to witnesses, the male driver was carried away limp from the vehicle and nobody got a good look at the assailants, but we do know that there were two of them. I'm just filling out a basic traffic incident report. That's all I can do right now because nobody even knows who the guy was."

"Melvin John Travis is who he was."
Mike saw the officer write the name down.

"Thanks. With that I can at least do a
missing persons report. Can you give me a
photo and description?"

"I'll have my office send you everything
you need."

"Nobody saw anything?" he asked in a
higher than normal pitch.

"Nothing other than that, Sir, and the
descriptions I'm getting are very generic."

"What about the type of car or color they
got away in?"

"The color of the car was white. Some
say it was big and some and some say it was
small, but most say it was big."

"Like a limousine or like a luxury car?"

Chris looked back at the man that he had
been talking to. "You, Sir, you said it was big.
Was it as big as a limousine?"

The small elderly man shook his head
and said, "No, Sir, it was more like a luxury car.
It looked like a big Cadillac to me."

"Which direction was it traveling?"

"South."

"That's at least something." Mike reached
into his right pocket, brought forth a card, and
handed it to the officer. "I'm an FBI special
investigator. My name and phone number is on

the card and I can be reached at anytime. I will need all of the information that you collect here. We will send somebody to pick up the car from the police impound yard."

"Yes, Sir, I'll make sure you get everything." The officer took his right hand away from the clipboard, unbuttoned his left hand shirt pocket, and removed a card. Handing it to Mike, he said, "The card has my badge number, precinct, and radio I.D. With this, you can get in touch with me anywhere."

Mike took the card and put in his left shirt pocket. "Thank you, Officer Green. I'll be in touch. Oh! One more thing... Keep my name and FBI out of any reports that you file."

"Yes sir."

When Mike turned, he pushed with his hands toward Sam and Peter. As he walked, he began muttering, "Dang it! There will be hell to pay for this."

6

Melvin's prone body lay on the linoleum floor. His face, flush to the cold surface, was pointed toward the back wall. Saliva from an open mouth dribbled down to a wet spot on the cement floor.

He fluttered matted eyelids and saw the blurred and dimly lit wooden chair in the corner of the room. Where was he? He rubbed the matter away from his eyes and noticed the bare plywood beyond. He put his right hand to the floor and flopped over.

Here he was, in a mess again.

The ceiling was bare plywood too. His head pounded with the force of a sledgehammer that he could feel in his temples and eyeballs. When he closed his eyes, he could feel that when his heart pulsed shooting blood through his veins, his head throbbed in unison. These were no regular heartbeats. It was amazing to learn that his frail human body could be radically affected like this. He moved both hands to his eyelids and rubbed, first with his fingers, then with the butt of his hand. What happened??? He was headed to the meeting just as planned and now this. *But what was this???*

He remembered stopping the car, fighting, and then everything went black. The rubbing hands were helping his head, but only marginally, so he sat up, moving the hands behind him for bracing. *Oooh!* The motions made his head throb worse. A shake of the head didn't help. It just made him dizzy.

He looked to his right and saw metal bars. Was he under arrest??? Where was Mike in all of this?

He managed to get to his feet and noticed that his head pain was starting to subside and he could now hear faint talk coming from around the corner. He could make out three distinct voices and one of the male voices was familiar. When the voices paused, he heard light footsteps coming his direction.

A thin woman walked into the room. She had the figure of a model, 36-24-36, perky lips, short rust-colored hair, and blue eyes that stared at him as she walked. "How are we doing?

Although her voice was sweet and melodic, Melvin knew that this was no time for pleasantries. *How dare they kidnap him?* "Whaddya mean, **'WE'**??? **'WE'** are not behind bars!!! I'm in jail and you're out there. How do you think I'm doing, *Miss*?!? I have missed a rendezvous that was supposed to have saved my true love's life!" Melvin stepped towards the bars and put his hands on them. As he did, the woman took two steps back.

The woman's face hung downward. "I know, and I'm sorry. We just couldn't let you give the FBI what they wanted."

Burning anger made Melvin stick his head between the bars. He wanted to charge at her, but the barrier between them made him settle for glaring at her with twisting white knuckles on the bars. The dull creak from the rotation was satisfying but the friction made his palms sweat and he could feel the sweat building. "What the heck do you mean???"

The woman took a step forward. With downcast eyes, she said, "I shouldn't have said anything. That's Rob's place."

Anger coursed through Melvin's body and his grip on the bars loosened. He took a step back for a moment. "DO YOU MEAN **'ROB MILGREW'**?!?!?" His could feel his eyes flare as he looked up and in all directions beyond the cell. "ROOOOOOB!?!?"

From down the darkened hallway, an older, tall, and muscular physique came in a fast walk. "What is it? What's going on???" As a figure trotted down the wide corridor, he shouted, "Is that you, Melvin?"

"*You're damn right it's me*!!! Come here you son of a bitch!" They had kept him from a meeting that would've saved Margie. These people were progeny's of humanity in all its feeble, erroneous, glory.

When Rob walked into the alcove, Melvin asked, "*How dare you jeopardize Margie's life like this*???" He pulled on the bars in front of him. The bars didn't rattle, but his body was jolted backwards and forwards due to the force.

Rob walked up to the cell and said, "Please calm down, Melvin. There's a lot that's happened that you don't know."

"*Yeah... I've heard that a lot lately*!"

"Yes, but I doubt that you have been told the truth about anything. At least not the *WHOLE* truth...." Rob looked over at the chair in the cell and pointed a finger towards the next room. "Why don't we grab some chairs and talk this thing through."

7

Melvin turned his head and saw the wooden chair sitting in the corner with its seat pointed towards him. In the flurry of the previous moments, he'd almost forgot it was there. He walked over to it, grabbed the top rung with his right hand, and jerked it away from the wall. With his bulging jaw locked shut, he carried the chair and set it directly in front of Rob who was already lowering himself into the chair that was brought to him.

Rob's chair was a fancy rolling one, plush, with brown padding at the back and tush areas. Melvin's bright red face grimaced as he plopped his butt down. The wimpy chair squalled under his modest 180-pound frame, the hard seat hurt his tailbones, and the arch of his back screamed at him. It figured! He put a hand to his back and rubbed. He would have been more comfortable sitting on a two by four.

Rob lifted his hand a bit. "I'm sorry for what you've been through. I'm especially sorry that Bruno put you to sleep. Waking up from that stuff isn't very pleasant, but at least it passes qui...."

"STOP! Forget about all that and just tell me what in *the hell* is going on. I mean, I thought everything was settled and then they kidnap Margie thinking I still have some stuff? *C'mon man!!!* Then the FBI break into OUR house and want to HELP ME get HER back in an effort to break up these groups that are doing the SAME research! Now, you kidnap m..."

Rob's right hand lifted up flush in front of him. "Easy... Relax... Take a breath.... We'll work through this."

"All I care about is Margie. Just get her back to me and then you can blow the whole world up for all I care." Feeling sweat appear on his forehead, Melvin swiped at it with his the back of his hand.

Rob raised an arm halfway. "Easy, Mel."

Melvin's back stiffened. "Don't call me that! You're not allowed!" He stood up and started circling the cell in a fast paced walk.

Rob motioned toward the chair and said, "Okay, Melvin. ... Will you please sit back down?!?"

Melvin jerked at the seat and the floor squalled again under the chair. "Behind bars?!?"

"*For now, yes.*" Rob's eyes glanced down. "Please?"

Melvin huffed and crossed his arms dropping them to his chest with a slight bounce. "Okay, tell me stuff!"

"Well, since we last saw each other, I've been working with the investigation regarding Senator Lucy Gold, but we found that there were no direct ties between her and Earth, Inc. That could only mean one thing."

"Who is Senator what's its?"

"Senator Lucy Gold was blackmailing Petry's assistant Nancy for information about time reversion. We thought she was the one who started the research."

Melvin leaned forward in his chair, unfolded his arms, and sighed. "That means someone else must be coordinating the research because of the disappearance of that investigator that Mike talked about."

"That's right, My Friend. ... Senator Gold was simply trying to cut herself in on the deal, presumably, to gain power."

Melvin head leaned back and his eyes widened. "WOW!" As his head righted, he asked, "So who is the mastermind?"

"We still don't know. The FBI found out through Earth Inc.'s records that some rich, power hungry guy named Reggie Van Heusen was the money-backer then, but now we don't know. The thing we suspect now is that there is a ring of labs researching the same technology. We don't know yet how many there are, but we have a lady on the inside who tells us that there are at least two more labs involved."

Melvin leaned forward in his chair once more, propping his forearms on his legs. "Gee.... They have got to be stopped! You know that huh?"

"Yes, they do, but if we attack the leadership group, the labs will splinter off and become independent, which we don't want. If we attack the labs, they will just start new labs."

"How are they all linked?"

"We think that they are all linked up through a private computer network by way of the Internet, but we don't know for sure."

Melvin felt an icy chill go up his spine. It appeared that the problem didn't get resolved, only delayed. "You can't let this go on, but it still doesn't answer why you kidnapped me?"

Rob took a deep breathe and exhaled through an open mouth. "No, it doesn't, and you deserve an explanation. ... First of all, we didn't kidnap you, but..." Rob leaned forward and put his hands on his knees "here's where it gets interesting. Melvin, have you ever known our government to do one decent thing?"

"No. Humans are a horrible species. They would sell their own mother just to get ahead."

Rob leaned back. His normally tan flesh turned white. "There was a time in my life when I believed in our government and the things that they did. I truly believed that following orders was the best thing to do, but that time is no more. Our government is as crooked as the worst criminal."

Melvin huffed. **"*You're a genius*!"**

Rob continued without hesitation, "The FBI team that was investigating you and the disappearance of Margie may be good men, but they are still following orders of corrupt people. Our government, specifically the vice president,..."

"The vice president???"

"Yes! She wants the technology for time reversion to control you, me, and everyone else. I was involved in building a case against the senator. I saw the sparkle in Alva Thornburg's eyes when we briefed her and President O'Reilly about the technology. A few days later, the NSA assistant director and I were having a meeting and while he was out of the office, I peeked at his computer and found confidential orders from Ms. Thornburg telling him to secure the technology *at all costs*. You're smart enough to know what *at all costs* means?"

Melvin nodded, but remained silent.

8

"Hey, this is Margie again. I still have my blindfold and ams tied up, but now they have put something over my ears that plays music. It's light jazz at least, Kenny G, I think.

I never thought I would be a damsel in distress, but here I sit. When I first met Melvin, he was so very alone like I am now. Not that he had to be, mind you, but because he wanted that life. A life alone.... I'm experiencing a little taste of that now and it's a cold and worrisome feeling. I am afraid for my life and Melvin's. The world hangs in the balance of what he does.

Right now, I know these people want the stuff we burned, but I don't know if poor Melvin has any help or would accept any help from anyone. He is more stubborn than ten thousand mules! *HA!* That is both for and against him. It won't let him give up on achieving his goals, but it also prevents him from listening to alternative ideas.

Bless him and dang him! I just hope he comes through for me. I think I hear something... Gotta go."

*

Melvin held his head propped on his right hand. Why did this all have to happen now? He had just found a little bit of happiness for the first time in his life. Damn the world anyway! Was everyone conspiring against him?

He looked at Rob, studied his wrinkled face, then folded his arms together. "So...???" He raised his hands expecting an answer. Without further explanation from Rob, he asked, "Why did you kidnap me???"

"Because if you still have Tom's research, we didn't want it to be used by the likes of our government and, if you didn't, we didn"t want them to kill you. That's exactly what would've happened too."

Rob was right of course and Melvin knew it, but he sure wasn't going to give them the satisfaction of knowing it. Something about this whole mess still didn't seem right. It was portrayed in the darkness, but right now, he wasn't in a position to argue. "I guess I should be thankful that you gassed me, huh?"

"Well, you were naturally fighting."

"Forget it," Melvin said with the wave of a hand. "How long have you been operating covertly?"

"About two weeks, but we're pretty well organized, at least, so far. This place is our command center. It's a refurbished underground bunker. It was re-done for the famed 2012 disaster that never happened.'" He chuckled. "Gotta love those disaster freaks."

"Well, how about my girl Margie? She is my only concern."

Rob put his hand to his chin. "Man, I don't know. I don't know where she is, how she is, or anything else. We don't even know if she's alive."

"Then what the frig am I wasting time here for?" Melvin felt a flame of anger shoot through his legs and he stood up. The wooden chair that he was sitting on tipped over behind him and made a loud crash as it hit the floor. He felt flush and a fleeting feeling of great loss shot through him. His arms dropped to his side then both hands balled up into fists. "I don't want to hear that! I'm telling you she's alive!"

Rob leaned forward. "Whether or not you believe me, I know how you feel, but these are the facts. The FBI doesn't even know. If they told you that they knew, they were lying. ... Don't trust the government, whatever you do..."

"Tell me something I don't know."

"Okay. We think that your wife probably is alive, but for how long we don't know. ..." Rob put his hands to his knees and slowly stood up. "Before I let you out, there is one thing that I have to ask you."

"Go ahead."

Rob leaned forward more and asked, "Will you help us?"

Melvin knew he needed time to think so he put his hand to his chin and rubbed. It was either trust Rob and his society or the government. Actually, he didn't trust either one. He only trusted himself, but Rob only asked for help, not trust. What kind of help did they want? It was an unknown factor and a moot point as long as he was trapped in this makeshift prison cell. To help anyone, even himself, he would first have to get out from behind these bars. He raised his head and said, "Well, I have never trusted the government and I definitely don't see any reason to start now. Yes, I'll help you, with the understanding that my priority is her."

Rob arched his eyebrows, leaned back, and parted his lips with a big smile that showed his pearly white teeth beyond. "I completely understand. Thank you, my friend. We'll need all the help that we can get." He looked over his left shoulder at the woman behind him. "Davina, please let this man out of the cage."

Melvin's head turned to Davina as she stepped forward grabbing the ring of keys from her belt line. She fumbled for the correct key, and inserted it into the lock. After a slight turn, it clicked. As she removed the key, stepping back with one of the cold bars of human cruelty in her hand she said in a low tone, "There you go, Melvin."

In a fit of bridled anger, Melvin's trembling hand pushed the bar as it moved. He sniffed the air of freedom, which was the right of every law-abiding, decent, person. When he was beyond the doors edge and was certain that he was truly free, Melvin asked, "So, Rob, what's the plan?"

"Let's go in here and talk about it," Rob said as he led them to the next room.

9

"I'll have their heads!" shrieked Senator Lucy Gold inside the Great Hall of her New Hampshire home. Her words echoed off of the twenty-foot ceilings and down the four endless fifteen-foot wide hallways. The many crystalline ornaments in the six-foot wide chandelier tinkled in their rebuke.

The five-foot-six young man in front of her waved his arms saying, "Be careful, Senator, they could easily have this place bugged!"

Lucy's red face looked down at the youngster. "You think I friggin' care about that?!?"

The lad lowered his hands, saying, "W... Well, the investigatio..."

"I don't care. I'll wipe them all out if I have to. They can't stop me and they know it. Money is power, Son, and I'm richer than the government."

The young man glanced down as he clasped his hands. "Well, Ma'am, you at least can't give them any kind of edge on you until you can use the time reversion safely."

The bulging jaws of Lucy's red face loosened and her tight narrowed eyes relaxed a bit. "I suppose you're right, Justin. You're a good aide." She took a breath. "At least I wiped one obstacle away. Trace Hooper had to go and you know why."

"Yes, Ma'am."

The rest of them will be gotten rid of on another day, especially that smarty pants lead investigator, Mike Curry."

"Shhhhh...."

"I don't care. Let'em come. I'll zap them all away."

"What about what I said. You need to be careful."

Lucy looked down at the lad. Her skin glistened with heavy makeup. She was fifty-years-old with no husband or kids. In fact, she had been quoted in a newspaper when she was in her thirties that if she had kids she'd kill'em. She then bought the newspaper's controlling company, fired everyone, and printed a retraction. The quoted statement was true, but it didn't fit with her idea of the kind of public image that she wanted.

She was rich by means of the computer and oil companies she had bought in her twenties. Her father, who was born into wealth, had loaned her the money to acquire the companies. She quickly gained the respect of business allies and gained the reputation of being ruthless without morality. Her controlling corporation, Mistress Gold, Inc., went to Microsoft stockholders, past and present, and did a hostile takeover.

Five years later, she nabbed Walmart, Inc. in the same manner. Proctor & Gamble proved to be too much, but IBM wasn't. After many failed attempts to acquire more companies, she wanted to change the laws that were annoyances to her takeovers. At the age of forty-three she ran for senator of Nevada and won.

"I don't tiptoe around," she said. "It's not in my nature."

Justin opened his arms wide. "I want you to keep calm, but, I have to tell you something."

Her eyes narrowed with tight lips. She tilted her head, looked down into Justin's squinting eyes, and with a calm voice asked, "What is it?"

Justin pulled his chin down, to refrain from looking directly at her, and cleared his throat. His arms folded halfway toward his chest. With splayed fingers bouncing as he spoke, he said, "There was a witness to Mr. Hooper's disappearance?"

Lucy's already pink face turned rose-red. Her brows arched. She paused a moment, put her hands at her side, and said, "Since Trace was wiped away from existence, this 'witness' shouldn't remember anything, right?"

"That's what we thought, but somehow he does, but outside of you and I, he's the only one, and we only remember from the chamber notes we wrote." Justin reached into his pocket and brought out a white paper and unfolded it. "That witness and this note, plus yours, is the only proof that this guy ever existed..."

"I know all these details.... We need to kill this witness. What's his name?"

"Matthew Craps."

Lucy chuckled, making her B-cup breasts jiggle. "Craps, huh? Well, Mr. Craps just rolled snake eyes."

Justin put a flush hand in front of him. "Not quite. He's disappeared. He's evidently talked and been tucked away somewhere."

Lucy's hands, fingers filled with diamond and other jeweled rings, bobbed up and down underneath her breasts as she said, "I'll find him and we'll get rid of him the old fashioned way."

"Yes, Ma'am."

Senator Gold paced around the room in a long-stride, fast walk. She put a right hand to her head and scratched between the red strands of hair. "I have no contacts within the FBI and

I'm not even sure where they would keep someone like that."

Justin, following her with body and eyes, said, "In a safe house, I suppose, but where is anybody's guess.

"I need to do some research into this."

10

Mike bolted into a near run as he approached the white van. His pitted face was expressionless except for tightly pressed thin lips and black-hair waving a bit from the icy wind. He stroked the hair down as he opened the side door.

There were two men sitting in chairs behind a light-gray metal desk filled with electronic gear. They both turned their heads and shuddered when cold air blew into the vehicle. Mike ignored the movements, stepped up into the vehicle, and closed the door.

"Hey, Boss, what can we do for you?"

Mike's head swiveled between the two men as he replied, "Roger is supposed to be here any seco...."

The van's side door swung open again and Roger leaped in. "Sorry, fellas."

"Alright, you two, out." Mike turned his palms up, extending the hands toward them, then swiping in the direction of the side door. The two men rose from their chairs, quickly grabbed their coats, and exited, pulling the door closed behind them.

After eyeing one another, both new men seated themselves. Mike pointed to the black headset lying in front of Roger as he picked up the other and slipped it over his ears. He fingered the foam on the microphone, reached for the panel in front of him, and started pressing buttons.

A deep female voice answered. "National Security Agency, Assistand Director Maywear's Office. May I help you?"

"Stella, this is Mike Curry with the FBI. Is Mr. Maywear available?"

"Hold on a minute, Mr. Curry, I'll check."

There was an almost inaudible click and then classical music. Mike put his right hand on the desk with and started drumming his fingertips.

Moments later, the phone clicked again, follow by a moderate male voice. "Charles Maywear here."

"Mr. Maywear, this is Mike Curry and Roger is here with me. We have a bad situation with regards to the special project."

Charles grunted. "What's the details, Mike?"

"Well, Sir, they captured Melvin's girlfriend and are holding her for ransom of the temporal materials, which Melvin has told me, have been destroyed. With limited time before the drop, we decided to do Ordinance 51 of the Hostage Code. Before he could get to the area, he, himself, was kidnapped. We still don't know by whom or why."

"I assume that you planted a GPS tracker?"

"Yes, Sir, but not knowing the situation, we were wait..."

"Need I remind you that this technology is of an extreme national security interest?"

"No, Sir. I completely understand the risks of time reversion."

"Well, then get this guy Melvin, at all costs. At the moment, he is our only link to these people."

"We were hoping that they would show up at the rendezvous point so that we could follow them, but no one showed up that we saw. I suspect that they were tailing him or, possibly, that they got him too and the drop-off was just a ruse."

"Mike, we've been friends a long time and I recommended you for this assignment. Don't make me regret anything. Use the damn GPS and go get this guy, and whoever the hell he's with. Most of all, get this technology! We need to secure it before it's used against us."

"Yes, Sir."

Mike heard a click in his ears and he knew that that meant Charles was angry. Possibly about the situation, but, more likely, at him for his reserved caution... He removed the headset off and laid it on the desk. Beside him, Roger did the same. The two looked at one another with raised eyebrows. "Well, we have our orders," Mike said.

Roger's eyes narrowed. "I just hope we are doing what's right."

"Our hands are tied. We have to go in *no matter who it endangers*. I'd rather wait to see what we're dealing with, but orders are orders. What more can I say? "

11

When Melvin walked into the next room, he saw three other exits. The corners of the room had shiny stainless steel supports. The white walls were smudged with dirt, grease, or some unidentifiable, dark shapeless spots of odd sizes. It made his stomach flip-flop. Keep your hands to yourself, Melvin thought. He saw a mahogany-textured table in the center of the room and made his way toward it since it was obviously their meeting place. It was round, which reminded him of the knights of Camelot, although these people certainly weren't as noble as those knights. They were more like thugs that thought they knew better than the common person how the world ought to be run, but if it would get Margie back, he'd play along. There were a number of rickety chairs pushed underneath and he recognized Rob's plush seat in the center of the other side.

"It's not much," Rob said as he put his arms to the chair and lowered himself, "but it serves our purpose well."

Rob was the big whale in this small pond of fish. Their operation was better than none and at least maybe their goal was worthwhile. Melvin huffed. They were serving their own self-absorbed goals though. It didn't really matter to him how perverse time reversion was anymore. He wasn't about to play their game. He wanted Margie back. That's it!

It's strange, he thought, how much a man can change in three weeks, well, four, including hell week. He had become a complete man and nothing was going to change that. It was Margie who made him that way. She had taught him that human kind was not all about greed, lust, and taking. He guessed that she'd always known that he was not a self-absorbed hypocrite and she proved to him that there were others besides him that there were others decent. Very few, but some... The seven deadly sins ruled most of humanity. It was only by miracles that some were left untainted.

He sneered at having to endure this "recruitment", but grabbed the plastic-backed chair in front of him, pulled it out, and lowered himself into the seat. Grabbing the front lip of his seat, he scooted himself, gut-tight, up to the table. There was a shrill cry as the metal coasters on the bottom of the chair scraped against the cement floor. Everyone else put hands to their ears or scrowled. It's what they deserved, but he wasn't about to say so.

The dim lighting was from a center fixture and it was dim enough to make everyone's faces look like some of the zombies from Late Night Horror on the Fright Network. It had been of his favorites as a teen. He and the other boys had to hide their watching of it from Linda, the foster home supervisor. She didn't like macabre things and kept a watchful eye to censor it from the household. The boys would take turns keeping her occupied to help the others enjoy. More often than not, it worked.

The dank setting here probably contributed to the mold or whatever it was on the walls although fluorescent lighting somewhat inhibited mold growth.

Rob's gray-fringe was bent over a tablet computer and some paper notes that lay on both sides of the table's surface. While he was sorting the materials, Davina and the others seated themselves with a multitude of varied scuffing noises.

Except for Rob and Davina, the faces in the room reminded Melvin of the rock band, Kiss, young, dark and angry. Although their originality was admirable back in those years, unfortunately, it was just as noteworthy how destructive their behavior had been, a human norm. The only exception was a largely built man sitting on Rob's left wiggling to an unheard tune and drumming his fingertips on the surface of the table.

Rob looked glanced at the burly guy. "Will you stop that, Bruno?"

The big guy snapped his head around. "Yep, sure will, Bro'." He stopped and laid his hands on the table.

"Thanks," Rob said. He turned his head toward everyone at the table momentarily pausing at each one's eyes as his head swiveled. When he locked eyes with Melvin, he spoke again. "Melvin, across from you is, of course, Davina Myers."

Davina waved her right hand and smiled.

"She comes to us from FBI headquarters. It was from her and I talking that we formed this group. We each knew that this technology had to be stopped and that our government was too corrupt to dispose of it on its own. To your left is my brother Bruno."

The large muscular figure pitched forward as he rose slightly from his chair. "It's a pleasure." He retook his seat.

"He is skilled in special weapons and tactics," Rob smiled and nudged him on the shoulder with a closed hand. "At my request, he took a leave of absence from the Miami P.D." Rob motioned with his other arm toward the man sitting left of Davina. "Last, but not least, we have Zac Thomas."

The salt and pepper headed man looked at Melvin, smiled, nodded, then turned back toward Rob.

"Zac and I met in the military and kept in contact over the years. He's our pilot with a private air strip not too far from here." Rob spread his arms in font of him. "None of us are married and no real attachments except for you Melvin. That makes you a liability, but all of us feel that you are a worthwhile risk. You see, we are a democratic organization and everyone here had to be voted in except for me and Davina."

"What about the others?"

"Weeeell," Rob stressed, "the others are part of our group with voting rights and each one is much appreciated with their special skills, but we four are the core with the necessary contacts to eradicate this techology."

... Geez, what rigmarole ... thought Melvin as he turned his head to look at the BIG four of them again. What in the hell had he gotten into? Secret societies usually exist because of what they stood for or against were all kinds of terrible reasons. It reminded him of the criminals that revolted, killed, and founded the

United States. They were criminal heroes, but still criminals.

He scowled letting his resentment be heard as well. Rob's stone face of pale wrinkles stared at Melvin and asked, "Is there a problem, Melvin?"

"I didn't want to join anything."

"Neither did we," Rob said, "but to get rid of this technology, we need to work as a team."

That much was true, but last time it nearly killed him and Margie both and he wasn't anxious for a repeat. He only got involved in this mess because Tom Soren wanted his help so what in the hell was he supposed to do? Turn down his only friend? That was last time though; this is now. He had found love. Recovering his lover and new best and only friend was the important thing, not this other world shattering bull. Melvin put both hands in front of him. "Whoa, Big Guy! I said I'd help, not join. All I care about is getting Margie safe."

"You don't have to join us, but the only way we can keep your girl safe is by eliminating the technology and the groups that are trying to use it."

Melvin slapped the table with both hands resulting in a loud thud. "*Eliminating*??? You mean by DESTRUCTION and MURDER?!?"

"If necessary, yes."

12

Bug-eyed, Melvin shook his head. "Geez, Man! Don't you think that's a little overboard???"

Rob's stone-faced stared at him. "No! When you consider the fate of everyone's lives hang in the balance... NO." Rob quickly put his hands to the table as he rose from his chair shaking his head. "Noooo!!! I'd do ANYTHING to save everyone from the uncertain demises that this can bring about."

Davina, arms by her side, leaned forward. "Rob, you know I'm with you, but you also know that I feel the same way as he does. The importance does not justify *any means necessary*."

Melvin snapped forward and unseated himself from the chair. His chair scraped the floor going backward when his stiff thighs bumped it. He put his hands on the table and he propped on them. His face, gorged with red blood. This was insane!!! He stared at Rob. "Listen, ya'll can do anything you want, but I will not help kill anyone. I am here for one thing: MARGIE. *Plain and simple*! You can blow one another to hell and back as long as you don't jeopardize her life. I'm officially out of the *save the world* bit."

Rob raised his hands and fanned the table. "Please, sit back down, Melvin. Nothing says that you have to join us and we won't ask you to do anything that you're not comfortable with."

Melvin arched backwards into a standing position. "Alright, just as long as we understand each other." Rob flashed the OK sign making Melvin feel a bit more at ease so he reached behind him with fumbling fingers and grabbed the seat of the orange chair. He pulled it back underneath his butt as he said, "Okay, so let's talk."

"Now that all of us know where we stand, Davina, what did your source say at the White House?"

There was a muffled thump overhead and everyone looked up. Rob snapped his head back down. Red-faced, he looked straight at Melvin with narrowed eyes. "Do you have a phone or anything electronic on you?"

Melvin's eyes grew wide and the color drained from his face. He lurched forward and lifted his butt from the chair. Stuffing a hand into his pocket, he grabbed his phone, brought it out, and tossed it onto the table. The dull hollow sound as it hit pierced the silence and the rocking reverberated off of the walls in the room. Melvin twisted his neck looking at white faces. Each person in the room was doing the same as he was, trying to determine what those faint sounds were. Everyone's eyes were as big as lighthouse beams with pupils that engulfed their irises. Melvin knew that this meant more trouble.

Rob stared at him a moment. The sudden silence was pierced by another thump. He looked at Davina and with the gruff voice of a badly running outboard engine said, "*Meeeeeellllvvviiiiiiiin...!*"

"I... I... I..." He could feel the heat of embarrassment burn his cheeks. His temples throbbed and he looked down from Rob's steely stare and his souled burned inside of him. He knew that anything electronic could be tracked, but was so focused on getting Margie back, that he had become lost in a pool of emotion. The ways of humanity were corrupting him. He had become the thing that he despised most: *a feeling person. **A human**!* "Damn it! Damn it! Damn it!!!" His hand, already balled up in his lap, rose and slammed into the table. When his fist bounced up, he opened the hand and slapped it against the side of his face. He saw Davina shudder either from his outburst or fear of what was coming.

"*Alert Code ONE*," shouted Rob as he shot up from his chair.

13

The padded brown chair freewheeled backwards about two feet, Rob pointed to Davina. "Take Melvin with you! Everyone else, you know what to do."

Davina shot up from her chair the rapidity of which made her rusty hair bounce from the tops of her shoulders. The others were already standing and staring at Rob. "Yes, sir," Davina squeaked out with a big airy breath. She leaned over and grabbed the top of Melvin's hand into hers and squeezed. Her blue eyes glared at him. "Listen up! For the sake of all of us, DON'T THINK, just do whatever I say. Do it quickly or we might all wind up dead."

When Davina released his hand, Melvin put both hands to the arms of the chair, pitched forward, and with low voice said, "Yes, Ma'am." He knew that he had committed a major mistake. He had compromised weeks of hard work setting up their headquarters. Their well-laid plans were being smashed into bits and all because he was too focused on a woman. A WOMAN!!! Of all things to have made him into simpering, distracted idiot...

How dare he take a cellphone with him in that friggin' car. He knew better than to trust anyone except Margie. As he rose to his feet, he knew that the only thing left to do was run. He turned toward Davina.

"Follow me," she commanded with an articulate voice as she grabbed her jacket and threw her arms in the sleeves. She spun around and started sprinting toward one of the hallway openings. Melvin burst into a run, following her lead.

The pair streaked through the white walled hallway twenty yards to the end where there was a teal curtain. Davina extended her right arm toward the left edge of the ruffles and pulled the cloth back about two feet. Beyond the fabric was a small corridor about three feet wide. It was dark and Davina put her left hand to the wall and flipped a switch. Three dim bulbs in the center of the ceiling lit up a hallway roughly fifty yards long.

Melvin stared down the corridor. What was down there? The bulbs barely lit the walkway and it looked like a dead end. He didn't want to be trapped down there.

"In," she whispered with insistence and a motion of her free arm. Melvin bent forward and went under her arm, then waited for her to drop the curtain and take the lead. He followed her to the end where she turned left into a long dark hallway. Immediately afterward, she screeched to a halt and flipped two light switches. The hall behind them went dark and the long hall lit up.

Melvin saw Davina burst into an all-out run whispering, "*Come on,*" and followed her lead. He could hear the clapping of her soft-soled shoes as they pounded the cement floor as well as his own. Five yards, ten, twenty, thirty, forty, ... air was beginning to be a precious commodity. She was slowing, gulping air, and although he was not terribly winded, it surprised him how much a near two-months hiatus of chasing down despicable bums, thugs, and deadbeats affected him.

Being a private investigator had kept him in shape, but after he and Margie had apparently solved this world-ending, doom-and-gloom mess, he never thought he would be doing this crap again. Humanities ways were so despicable.

As soon he caught up with her, he patted her on the back. "Breathe," he said in an almost silent whoosh of air. She pulled her head up with squeezed eyelids and put a lone finger to her lips.

With a shake of her fist, she stretched her upper body forward and re-took a commanding lead. Melvin had begun wondering how long the tunnel was, having grossly underestimated it, until he squinted and saw a dark-gray wall ahead. The pounding of their steps grew louder in his ears. They were the drumbeats of his past and future coming to make his life a living hell again. Why? Why him? What did the three fates have against him?

What was the name of that book on Greek mythology? He couldn't remember, but he did remember the three fates. Clothos was supposed to spin the thread of life. Lachesis, the measurer, was the one who was supposed to choose the lot in life one will have and measures how long the thread was. Atropos, who at death, with her shears cuts the thread of life. Not even the gods wanted to mess with them. They actually pre-dated the gods.

Right now though, Melvin wanted to bash their heads in. How dare they mess with his life? He opened his mouth to scream, but clamped it down immediately causing the left incisor to bite into his tongue. Damn it! He could feel a pock-mark and the putrid taste of blood that was seeping into every crevice of his mouth. Fuck the world! Damn Lachesis, she predetermined his role in this, but he hoped and prayed for a long life to enjoy with Margie.

He saw Davina plant her feet to stop a short distance from door, but her feet skid making a sifting gravel noise as she skid face-first into a black wall. He heard the loud thump and planted his water-colored tennies to not suffer the same fate. She'd fallen to the floor, but was already using both arms to try and get to her feet again. Melvin grabbed underneath her left arm to try to help her, but Davina, after a moment, pushed him away with an angry scowl.

It was certainly a rude thing to do. He was only trying to help. Davina put a finger to her lips when he huffed. He should've known better, but he did it before realizing it.

She put a hand to her face and rubbed, then stepped to the left side of the door. There was a hinged panel that she lifted, revealing a light-blue backlit keypad. The screen was digital with yellow lettering that read, *Access Code:*. Davina moved her right hand to the keypad and started typing. In a few moments, the screen changed to, *Door Code:*. She typed a bit more and then a loud metal-click sounded and then there was a near-silent clack sound. After a moment, there was another clack and Davina moved to her right. She grabbed the metal wheel, and turned it several times, after which she pushed the door open and stepped through.

Melvin eyed the three-inch thickness of the door as the sunlight peeked through and lit up his chest. Looking beyond the door, he saw a flared cement exit like that of an aqueduct. His face felt the icy cold of February, but his nose smelled the definite clean of moisture in the air. Louisiana was humid, but not this humid. There had to be a river or creek nearby....

14

"Mike! Mike!" Roger pounded his feet as he ran in Mike's direction. There were several men around him in the clearing and each was wandering about with pulled pistols. The order was not to shoot unless fired upon and Mike knew he had been explicit.

He raised his right hand high into the wind and pressed the index finger of the other hand to his lips. He squinched his eyes and started walking in Roger's direction. He couldn't help but shake his head realizing his other order for the day, silence, was a moot point now. When he saw Roger look his direction, the arms went down.

The two men met midways, just beyond the other agents. Mike's tall figure stood two-inches above Rogers. His leathery skin and pot marked face was pale. He knew that they were going to be trying to sail against a hurricane wind if they lost track of their only lead.

"What's so important that you needed to shout???" he asked in a raspy, hushed, voice.

Roger tilted his head downward and in a significantly quieter voice said, "Well, Sir, the GPS coordinates of the phone are right where we're standing. I don't get this at all."

Mike's eyes widened. "Well, they're certainly not here. ... Are you sure?"

"Yes, Sir, and its not moving"

"There must be some mistake. There's nothing here but scrub brush." With a snap of his fingers, he pointed to the ground. "There can only be one answer: underneath us."

Roger's wide-eyed face was expressionless, but, nevertheless, he nodded.

Mike cocked his head and, after a moment, he said, "Roger, hurry and check the backup locator."

Roger smiled. "Aye, aye, Sir." He quickly jogged away in the direction of the black sedan.

The area was nothing but flat land, just weeds and dirt, not even a tree or bush. The harsh winter months had laid dormant the green grass that would normally lie on the sandy dirt surface. Now, it was a shadow of semi-crunchy hay and only in spots. The specs of brown shifted a bit with each of Roger's pounding footsteps. As his toes dug in to catapult him forward, sprays of dirt curled and flew into the air.

He grabbed the sedan door's handle and pulled hard. Roger leaped inside. He stretched his body, putting a hand on the driver's seat to brace himself and grabbed a four-inch square, one-inch thick, black device off the passenger seat. He exited the car and turned the screen toward his face then burst into a top speed run toward Mike.

When Roger neared him, he said, "He's running North."

Mike waved his hand and turned a circle, "Everyone, come here." The six men and two women ran toward Mike. "Alright, listen up. Our guy is running North. We need to cut him off." Mike pointed at four of the men. "You four go due north with me. Roger," he said as he pointed, "you'll take the rest and circle around to the west and try to get ahead of them. I'll radio you if they change directions and I'll get a helicopter in here too. Go!"

15

Two people had Margie's arms looped under theirs. By the salty, moist scent permeating her nostrils and the warmth of rough skin with its soft hairs brushing lightly on her body, she assumed they were men. She still had a mask on and her arms were fastened behind her back with some kind of cold metal that she assumed to be handcuffs. With her mouth still stuffed with some kind of rubber gag, she couldn't manage a word. Not that she would have said anything anyway, except maybe cuss words, but she thought it never wise to annoy mad men.

She was thankful that they had uncovered her ears. Whatever they had put had been pinching her ears ever since she was thrown into the back of wherever vehicle they had. They'd not wanted her to hear anything probably out of cautious fear. Regardless, she was delighted to be able to move even if it was only a tiny bit. Once her ears were freed, it took a few minutes for them to stop throbbing. Now, she was here, wherever *here* was.

The only thing she had heard since had been the clops of shoes against a tile floor until the man to her left issued his commands,

"Walk here. ... Turn this way. ... Step here." She appreciated not being dragged everywhere, but the near silent monotony began to create an awareness in her of what a grave dilemma she was in.

Unfortunately, her position had been reduced to a blinded and helpless woman.

When they entered the next room, there was a slight delay between her marching orders. The paced slowed and finally she heard the word, *Stop*.

"You wanted to see her, Boss - here she is," a deep voice said to her left.

"Fine, fine, just sit her down right here," another voice said from in front of her. This one was definitely more of a low-tone, like a crisply enunciated crooners voice from back in the forties and fifties, Dean Martin-ish. "And for God's sake, take that *thing* from her mouth! We're not heathens here."

Margie felt something being done behind her head. She heard the jingling of metal and then the ball started to come out of her mouth. When her saliva dripped out, she gagged and thought she was going to puke but fortunately not. She immediately began limbering her jaw and mouth. After a few purses of her lips, she elevated her voice and demanded, "WHO ARE YOU???"

"It's best that you don't know that. I want to tell you how sorry I am that we had to involve you."

"Kidnappers never win, you know. *Bad NEVER triumphs over good.*"

The man cleared his throat. "Been watching movies, eh? Who's to say who is good or bad? Reality doesn't sell, Honey."

"Maybe not," she said, "but you will be sought. My Melvin will tear you apart."

"Perhaps. ... It wasn't supposed to be like this." The man gushed air. "You see, we were never planning to keep you this long. This was supposed to be a simple exchange, but it's gotten out of hand." He paused to clear his throat again. "Your man is merely a victim of time. Anyway, we don't know where he is or even who he's with."

"Oh?"

"Yeah... Whether he's gotten lost on purpose or not is also something we don't know."

"Then why do you say he's a victim of time?"

"Because he is the way he is because of unfortunate events in his life."

"Unfortunate things happen to everyone. Look, I know him and I know he'll turn up. He's a survivor," Margie said as she heard him stirring by the sounds of his padded seat shifting.

"Please believe me," he said with an air-ish, strained voice, "we have no intent on harming you or making you uncomfortable in any way. The way Melvin Travis is, we knew that he would never help us voluntarily. You know that as well as we do. ... We're treating you this way for your protection... not OUR's!"

Blah, blah, blah, Margie thought but did not voice although she couldn't help but take a deep breath.

"God, I AM SO VERY SORRY! All of us are very peaceful people that love this world, but realize that it could change for the better. "

Margie could hear a terrible anguish in the crooning voice that had became breathy. These men didn't seem cold blooded. "Listen you seem like a relatively nice guy, other than the obvious felony. Why not let me go..."

"I can't! There is so much potential good in this technology that we have to follow through. Besides, it's not up to me alone." The voice took a deep breath. Clearing his throat, he burst into a rendition of *It's now or never*' He didn't do a bad job, but it was a bit raspy. "I'm betting that you need a bathroom and something to eat. We'll make arrangements for all of that. For your sake, I'll use the name Boss and these two gentleman are Heckle and Jeckle. ... Say *Hi* you two."

The deep rumbly voice, "I guess I'm Heckle."

"I guess that would make me Jeckle, Ma'am," a higher crackly voice to her right said.

"You're not the head person?"

"Lord no! ... You're worldly enough to realize that everybody answers to somebody else, but we'll discuss that later. ... Okay, Boys, please make this attractive lady more comfortable."

Heckle put his arm underneath hers and pulled left. "Come this way, My Dear, and we'll get you set. Please don't try anything."

After she had been a short distance, he spun her around and she could feel him grab at her left wrist. Click! Something dropped with the jingle of metal, and brushed her mid-thigh. Her knee jerked forward.

"That's just the handcuff, Sweetie. I'll be done in a second. By the way, Miss, it'd be no use in trying to escape because the blinder requires a key to remove. I'll need to put the gag back too after we get you settled. So sorry, Ma'am, but it'll protect us all." His warm hand pulled the free wrist to the front of her body. Heckle grabbed her right wrist removing one set of bindings and replacing them with another.

Heckle placed her wrists a foot apart and said, "This is as much wiggle room as you have, but it should be lots more comfortable than being bound behind your back."

Margie sighed.

"All of us are very sorry that you have be here under these conditions. The gag and blindfold are for your protection so that, whatever happens, you are not involved with our group even though we are trying to do good. ... The world is a place of wickedness that starts at the top and trickles down. We want to help. Forgive us for what we must do. ... Now let's get you settled."

Heckle talked incessantly about "the good" of their operation while getting her set up in her room. He seemed so nice that she found herself empathizing with him and the truthfulness of his sorrows at having to keep her in her demise. The intense caring on Heckle's part, made somehow made her excuse his actions when he apologized over and over. He told her of his life and how his son was born with one leg and how that could possibly be corrected with this technology. *I'd do anything to make his life better*, he said. *That's why I joined up.*

Margie couldn't help but feel compassion.

16

Melvin followed Davina away from the aqueduct and began rubbing his hands together. With head lowered, he parted his mouth slightly and exhaled onto entwined fingers in warm hopes as Davina walked to the edge of the aqueduct. She looked from side to side contemplating. It seemed to him to be a waste of time, but he paused with her. In an instant, a foggy mist rose up around the sides of his face. It was cold too and now he wished that these people would've kidnapped his jacket too.

When she started moving to the right, he did too with strict attention to where she stepped, remembering about the possibility of booby traps. Looking ahead, he saw a river of some sort. It appeared to be about twenty yards away and wide. It didn't look deep or swift, but icy cold for sure. The trickles that were coming from it were a soft noise, but the sounds rattled his eardrums and, after only a few minutes, he just wanted it to go away ...by whatever means... He had heard stories about how people had been driven insane by the constant wind of the mid-west. Never having been there, he had to rely on the rumors, but suspected that it was something like the old Chinese water torture was supposed to have been.

Water boarding was an entirely different thing. During Chinese water torture, the victim is strapped to a chair and drops of water were dripped down on top of the head until it drove you insane. Over the years, people had made it equal to water boarding and it wasn't.

During water boarding you were strapped to a table and, with a thin cloth over your head, water was dripped into your nostrils giving the sensation of drowning. It could induce heart attacks, vomiting, even death. Only the military uses it and only on terrorists and prisoners of war. Whoever created time reversion needed to be done that way.

This was a mess that was of Tom's cohorts doing. The frustration of trying to undo it was making Melvin's hands quiver. He imagined that Davina considered his shaking was from the cold. It was chilly with a brisk wind, but his frustration and anger was what was burning deep in his soul.

As he looked up from Davina's footsteps, he saw they were headed towards the river, but at an upstream angle. The trek down to the riverbank didn't take long and the sandy mud of the bank reminded him of simpler times at the orphanage on those rare days of picnics at the creek. This river had the same gray and white rocks scattered about like this one in its two-foot wide strip. Those days were long past, but the fleeting thoughts of happier times made him smile for a moment.

Davina pointed. "Get in!" she commanded.

"In there?!? In the river?!?" Melvin tried to quietly shout.

"YES!!! Do you want to live?!?" she whispered.

The simple answer to that was an obvious yes, but to submerge himself in frigid water was ridiculous. He was no fool. He remembered from high school science that water was a great conductor and would draw what little body heat that he had to it. He didn't want to be a popsicle! He would be as cold as a witch's tit in there... but live... Hell yes! Live versus freeze ... easy decision.

He stepped off the bank into the mud. Unfortunately, it was not as firm as he had hoped: his foot sank two-inches. He trudged on until he was knee deep in brown water followed by Davina. It was stinging cold, setting his nerve endings on fire, buzzing his skin like angry bees.

He let out a series of "ooh's" and "aah's"

before Davina beat on his back with a knuckled fist and whispered, "Be quiet or I'll kill you myself." She moved beside him and glared a moment. Pressing a finger to her lips, she took the lead.

Melvin was looking at Davina's backside now, thinking that he was going insane from the simple noise of an icy brown river slapping his and Davina's legs. His feet were ice cubes and the blue-jean pants were sticking to his legs. Women were lucky enough to wear those light polyester things. Almost all men's pants were cotton, most prominently jeans for blue-collar working stiffs like him, which were heavy.

The two of them were only three-feet into the river, but it was still two-feet of water, plus two-inches of soggy bottom.

In a matter of minutes, Melvin's feet grew numb. A guy could lose a foot like this. He stopped a moment, looked up, and whispered to himself, "Lord, don't let me stumble." Trudging onward, he couldn't help but eye Davina's tight, round, derriere' in a form fitting black pair of polyester slacks. He shook his head a few times. This was not the time or the place to think such things. Besides, there was Margie to think about.

The two had been going upriver for about five minutes when Melvin suddenly grabbed the back of his left thigh. He rubbed the leg with one hand and put the bulk of his weight on the other.

Davina turned around in the water and sloshed back to Melvin. Eyeing his rubbing, he nodded. Melvin looked up and nodded as well and looked down at his body. His leg muscles felt like they were locked in a vise and he was mentally cursing himself as a weak bastard.

Davina's chin jutted upward as she looked behind them both at the motionless trees. "Shit! They found us!" Her voice was but a whisper, but full of air. "I don't care if you're dying, keep up, or ELSE!"

17

Senator Lucy Gold was about to walk into the chamber when she caught Justin walking toward her out of the corner of her eye. She immediately planted her feet causing Senator Dan Robertson, who was walking behind her looking down at the papers in his hand, to bump into the back of her shoulder.

"Excuse me," he said as he stumbled. He managed to right himself by bracing against the hallway wall. As soon as his legs were steadied, he looked up and saw her. "Well, I'll be. Lucy, I thought maybe since you were under investigation that you would be laying low?"

Lucy smiled. "Well, I'm not worried. Innocent people don't." She chuckled and spread her hands apart. "Look around you. Half the people around here are under investigation for something."

The portly man chuckled and said, "Yep, that's for sure." He nodded and then walked off.

Lucy turned toward Justin and, with a wave of her arm, and said, "I can tell by the look in your eye that something's up. What's is it?"

He frowned, then in a hushed voice said,

"We need to talk in private."

She smiled and pointed. "Certainly, Dear. Let's go down the hall. I think there's a cloak room that we can use." The two walked side-by-side thirty-feet down the wide hallway. Lucy tipped her head and smiled at everyone in the busy area.

After a number of twists and turns, Lucy entered a four-foot doorway. The large room beyond was well-lit from the fluorescent fixtures on the ceiling. Yeah, President Moron made them change every last government light to these putrid bulbs. She never liked them, but what're you going to do with morons that have power?

A plethora of suit and winter coats hung on hangers, lining the walls of the eight-feet room. Lucy loved these closets because of their built-in soundproofing. She turned and closed the mahogany door, then looked around the room, behind the coats, and underneath everything before turning toward Justin who hadn't uttered a sound.

Her head finally turned back towards the door once more, then she looked Justin directly in the eyes. In a hushed voice, she asked, "Okay, what's the deal?"

Justin looked slightly below her eyes to avoid her steely gaze. "I found out through FBI contacts that Melvin Travis doesn't have the materials for the temporal wall anymore. By his own admission, he has destroyed them."

"When???"

Justin shuffled his legs. "I don't know. Your source, Fred Gramsley, told me this."

"As FBI director, he should know." She pondered the news a moment, then started to say something, but Justin cut her off.

"Pardon me, Ma'am, but there is still more."

Lucy stared at the young man with hands moving to her hips. She spoke once again, sharply. "Yes!"

Justin took a step back with one foot. He saw his boss lady's face turn red and knew what it meant. He owed her his life a dozen times over for her rescuing him from the jaws of death and paying for his needs ever since she had found him as a six-year old child. He didn't really know where he came from or who his parents were. The only things that he knew for sure were that she saw him wandering the downtown streets of New York with nothing but the clothes on his back. After asking some questions, which he had none of the answers to, she gave him a ride to a small house occupied by an older couple. They treated him as a son and she would come by every now, visit for a few minutes, and hand over money for his needs.

When he graduated high school, she told him to major in political science at the University of Massachusetts so that at the end of it all, he could work for her. She hadn't ever done anything but help him so he did as she instructed without ever looking back. Now, he had to be the bearer of bad news, a position he did not ever like. "Mr. Gramsley also told me that this FBI team were snatched away from him and are now reporting directly to NSA assistant director Charles Maywear."

Lucy's right arm approached her face and, with nimble fingers, started rubbing her chin with only the tips. The shimmer of her orchid lips pulled down at the tug of her long nails. "I have a slew of contacts, but not a single one in the NSA." She turned her head and looked toward the door a moment then turned back at Justin's waist. "My friend, it may be time for Mr. Maywear and I to have a chat," she said as she lifted her head and looked into Justin's eyes.

He nodded and replied, "Indeed it is. What about Melvin?"

"Wait and see. He may be useful to us yet."

18

Melvin couldn't feel his feet anymore. Instead, he was trudging the nearly freezing water of the river with a couple of frozen bricks for feet. Worse still, just as he could sense relief on the way when she started to angle toward shore, he heard people following them. Davina's head turned. She must've heard those noises too. Oh, woe is life. These dreaded beasts called humans... Greedy Bastards! They had the morals of a snake. Self, self, self.... Although he had to live with them, he sure as hell didn't like them. Any of them! Except Margie...

In front of him was Davina walking through the frigid water the same as he was. He felt like cussing at her to get out of this wretched river, but he knew that would probably not do a bit of good. If he died, it would be a result of her orders and she would have to live with that. He smiled. It would serve her right. He didn't want to be caught. To keep their damnable secrets he knew that they were both scum on the soles of their shoes. They might be useful but all they really were was garbage. The more distance they put from the bunker, the louder the noises became.

Melvin eyed Davina as she looked all around.

She stopped, turned around, looked at him with a steely gaze, and whispered, "It's YOU!!! It has to be!!! I should've thought about it sooner! ... Okay, Dude, STRIP!"

"Strip! You mean to take my clothes off!!!"

"Not so loud," She stressed then nodded. "That's right, Honey, off with them! ... and I mean it! Everything!!!"

Melvin shook his head, but lowered his voice. "In this weather!!! You're crazy!!!"

"I don't have time to argue. Strip or take your chances!" Melvin paused and Davina starting walking away.

"Okay, okay, you win." Melvin grabbed the crease of his shirt and ripped. The white buttons flew off exposing his hairy chest and the shirt fell to the water, slowly drifting downriver.

"Submerge everything deep."

He shook a fist at her. Davina shoved a finger to her lips and Melvin clamped his jaw. He undid his pants and stooped deep in the water, pushing the cloth. When he started to walk again wearing only his Froot of the Looms and essentials, Davina twirled her finger, then began to march on. Glancing backward she whispered, "Come on! All of it!"

A movie title flashed into Melvin's head, *The God's Must Be Crazy*." Geez! It was crazy insane to get naked in this weather, but to pacify the lady, if you could call her that, he slipped his underwear, shoes, and socks off. He immersed himself near totally, his flesh stinging all over, pushing the clothing downward into the river hoping this hussy was happy now. His near frozen feet were feeling the pricks, prods, and squishes of the river's naked bottom. Lord only knew what all was else was in this river.

This was indeed a woman, her shapely body gave that away, but she was tough as nails. Margie was in unknown hands and these people knew who it was so he folded his arms around his torso as best he could and walked on. Anything for her... Damn all of this anyway! His skin was being set afire from the icy water below and wind above. This was purely fucking crazy. Sure, he wanted to live, but was this ordeal really worth the pains? He wasn't, but Margie was.

Davina walked on a good ways before stepping on shore where she stood comfortably clothed, motioning one arm at him to hurry. There he was ... standing in about five-inches of water and literally freezing his nuts off with his arms wrapped like a second skin as far as they could reach and she wanted

Him to hurry. Geez! He felt like shouting, *Take Your damn clothes off and come out here with me, you Hussy*! Instead, his temper was mitigated by the threat of *God knows what* behind him so he hurried along as much he could.

After several more steps, his muddy feet were on the sandy bank. He didn't know which was worse, the near freezing water or the icy wind on his weiner. Willie was turtling and screaming at him. Davina stood there hurrying him along, apparently uncaring about his misery, pointing to a trail between the trees and over the levee, turning towards it, and there he was waddling behind her trying to protect himself. After dropping his left hand between his legs, he discovered it didn't work like he had hoped because the protection was just as cold as the air. Fortunately, the trail's path was fairly smooth, but Melvin was feeling every prod, poke, scrape, and ouchie as if it were a spiked bed. "*Why me, Lord*," he muttered.

Beyond the crest of the levee, he saw a narrow country road and a navy-blue car parked alongside. Davina's auburn hair bounced as she ran to the driver's side door. Along the way, she brought up the keys from her pocket. They were securely nestled in her hand by the time she reached the door. She quickly inserted the prepared key and unlocked the doors.

Melvin's painful misery had turned to a sane madness. His only mission right now was warmth. All else didn't matter. His leaps down the hill were unstable with a few tumbles that were quickly rectified. Each falter embedded rocks, pebbles, sand, and twigs into his feet and body. With his masculinity cradled in an icy hand, his shoulder bounced into the passenger door. Just one more bad thing about today, he thought. As soon as he heard the click, he hurried into the vehicle. As fast as he could, he softly pulled his door closed. His counterpart did the same.

"Go, go, go!" Melvin called out from a near fetal position as she cranked the engine. Davina slammed the gearshift into drive and pulled onto the road.

"You realize this just make things worse, don't you?"

He looked at her and nodded. "Yes, but at least we're out of there for the time being." He bent his head down and looked at his groin. His prized jewels were drawn in as much as possible and his appendage, the poor little guy, was, limp, shriveled, and hiding. "Poor Willie. You don't like the cold, do you?" he said shivering.

Davina turned her head to the highway

when he looked up. "*Oh, Brother,*" she jeered. "We're in big trouble."

19

"This is Margie again. Well, whoever
Boss is, he did exactly as he said. Heckle and
Jeckle removed those tight bindings and fed
me something. It tasted like a cheap breaded
chicken TV dinner with green beans and some
fries. At least, I think they were fries, but I
never like any kind of microwaved potatoes.
They always taste like cardboard to me. I know
that I must have looked like an oinky pig, but
wearing a blindfold makes everything hard.

As I ate, nobody said a single word, not
that I cared. I was too starved to bother with
conversation. I've always been one of those
breakfast eaters. I never miss the occasion to
eat eggs, toast, grits, sausage, cereal, bacon, or
whatever else there may be on the menu. I love
my juice too, especially orange juice.
Nutritionists always write that breakfast is the
most important meal of the day. I always
repeated this when asked about my breakfast
obsession, but the reason is that my stomach
bothers me if I don't begin the day by eating
and, needless to say, I was deprived of filling
my stomach this morning.

Anyway, it didn't take me long to finish,
but afterward I heard them cart the water glass

and empty container away, Heckle told me to open my mouth. I didn't really want to, but did anyway. He put the gag back into my mouth. The front ribbing now covers my lips and most of my chin, separating my teeth about an inch and the bulb-end extends halfway into my mouth. Fortunately, it doesn't push against my tonsils. My head bobbed when I heard them snap it shut, but I couldn't help it. I didn't want that totally trapped feeling, but couldn't prevent it. When I flinched, he warned me not to try anything, but heck, where was I going to go?

Thereafter was the clicking sound of a lock. I think the sound of it, that metallic click made me wonder how prisoners tolerated being locked up. I mean just knowing freedom was gone. Oh, Melvin, where are you?

The guy led me a few steps, put headphones back on my head, and then I felt a pull on my wrist and shoulder urging me downward. As I lowered onto the floor, I stretched out my hands and felt a cold draft followed by the touch of brisk carpeted cloth. At least I wouldn't be terribly cold, but my pink satin nightgown and bare legs were no match for the cool drafts of February.

As I stretched my legs out and tried to attain a propped position for whatever duration, I felt a blanket thrown onto me. It began to warm my body instantly and, suddenly, my insides calmed from their quivery state to one of relaxation. Oh, how I wish Melvin were here. The only real security, other than with my parents, that I've ever known was with Melvin and they died a few years before I was married. Melvin brought security to my life.

He'll rescue me. I know he will. If I could only bring the secure comfort to him that he brings to me, our relationship would seem fair. Oh Killer, where are you? "

*

Margie was listening to the music coming from the headphones once again. She had always loved music, especially modern jazz, but, right now, she wanted to get away from it. She wanted the comfort of warm, strong arms but didn't know any way to get there. She was powerless. Loss of control was new to her as she'd always been the master of her own destiny. It was her right and responsibility as an independent person. A feeling of being helpless is evidently what they wanted to instill, but why was Boss talking to her? Why were these villains so concerned for her? Villains were bad people that didn't care about anything except their goals, but life was not like the movies.

They were simply a dramatization of life events. There was some truth in them and she had assumed that villains being bad guys were self-affixed to whatever they wanted and didn't care about anything but themselves. These people were totally inconsistent with that dogmatic view.

She adjusted the over-sized padded cups around her ears, but didn't try to remove them because, for one thing, she was assuming that they were locked in some fashion and, for another, and it was assured to be in her best interest not to hear anything. She chuckled as her brain flashed the image of the three wise monkeys from Japan: see no evil, hear no evil, speak no evil.

She was better off not knowing anything. If she could potentially identify them, they would kill her.

Suddenly, she felt the air stir on her left side. The headphones spread, then lifted away from her ears.

"Hello, Margie. I wanted to take some time and talk to you. I want you to know that we're trying to do good here."

It was Boss's deep crooner voice.

"Ma'am, I just can't tell you how very badly I feel about having you here for such a long time."

"Oh, yeah, Bub, well, then release me."

"I am at odds with myself. I don't believe in doing any harm to anything and while we're not doing any physical harm to you, there are long-term emotional effects of what you're going through. I am sorry that you have to be our guest."

Guest??? Guest was a far cry from this. You don't gag and bag guests, well, not unless you're kinky. Kinky was meant for fun. This was the opposite of fun and she couldn't help but shake her head slightly. It happened before even realizing what she was doing and she stopped immediately. When you're held hostage, it's generally much better if you don't piss off the kidnapper.

The deep voice rose in volume and pitch. "You don't think we've been fair to you???"

Oh no! Here it comes.

Boss's voice resumed its normally calm pitch. "Well, I don't blame you. ... From your perspective I guess we're all evildoers bent on getting our way. We're actually trying to rescue the world from itself."

Okay, that was unexpected. Usually bad men's first reaction to almost anything contradictory was anger.

"I certainly hope to convince you that we have good motives in using this technology.

We want to do I know there's a downside too, but isn't there always good and bad in everything?"

Margie heard a creak and the rustling of clothes.

"Assuming your boyfriend stays gone, I aim to show you that we can make the world a much better place. ... And just so you know, nobody knows where he is, not even the FBI. It seems as though he's deserted everyone. ... Pity."

20

It was high noon before Mike arrived in Washington. He had called Charles Maywear from Louisiana, but the NSA assistant director wanted him to brief the president in person so he quickly boarded a Model 36 Learjet parked in Baton Rouge's airport and took off. The eight-passenger cabin seemed lonely during the almost three-hour flight, but he was too consumed with trying to figure what the next step was to let it bother him much. When he landed at the Ronald Reagan Airport, he was met by two black-suited men who escorted him to a limo.

Now, here he was, on his way to meet the most powerful man in the world who was going to ask for a plan to deal with this mess. Mike's trouble was that he didn't have a clue yet what to say. His army training sure didn't prepare him for this. In fact, nothing did. The technology that they were trying to corral was unlike anything that anybody had ever experienced, except him.

He supposed it was precisely that reason why he and his team had been sent on this mission to begin with. The risks of involving anyone else were just too great and he, at least, had a basic understanding of what was going on. The president and his staff could be trusted, of course, but if an unscrupulous glory seeker found out about it, developed, and used it, then goodbye reality, and hello topsy-turvy.

Mike patted his black wool trousers at the pocket level with both hands and the agent to his right turned and looked. "Sir, may I ask what you're doing?"

As he reared back and stuck his hand into the pocket, Mike said, "Don't mind at all. I'm just looking for some peppermint."

The black-headed agent huffed. "Southerners...."

Mike took the wrapper off the candy and threw it into his mouth. "Hey, Pal, this ain't the '60's anymore."

The agent looked over at him briefly, looked away again, and then said, "Sorry."

The taste of the peppermint was soured by the rude remarks. The black limo was beginning to go down the driveway of the White House. Mike had never been here before and his gut was trembling slightly. The building was truly magnanimous with its wavy awnings and curved pillars. He couldn't help but be inspired, thinking about the laborious hours and high-level of skill that it took to create such a place as a symbol of the freedom and prosperity of a great nation. Maybe that was the point. The craftiness might've thought to have invigorated minds and help forge creative solutions. If that were true, he was in the right place.

The vehicle stopped in front of the building where he was escorted by an agent into the west wing. Outside the closed Oval Office door stood Charles who smiled and waved.

Charles was an instantly recognizable, semi-portly man of five-foot-six, two-hundred pounds, with a beer gut. It didn't stick out far, but hung there over the brown belt of a navy suit. When Mike got near, he smiled, and swung his arm like a side-armed quarterback throwing a long pass. "Charlie! You son of a gun! It's nice to see you."

Charles Maywear shook the hand, raised a finger to his lips. "Shhh! He's in there. I was early and he had to take a call, but he also said it wouldn't be long. Did you come up with anything?"

Mike eyes cast downward for a moment while he looked at his fidgety hands. "Well, I..."

The office door swung open. Standing inside the office was President Draven O'Reilly. His grayed head was atop a tall, but slim figure and the bright blue eyes that looked directly at Mike's. "Gentleman, thank you for your patience. Please come in," he said in a raspy voice. He took a few steps on navy-blue carpet and sat down on the sofa putting an open hand out toward the facing sofa saying, "Please be seated."

Mike admired the elaborate detailing on the Resolute Desk and looked down at the Eagle clutching arrows and an olive branch on the floor before he followed Charles to the sofa. What in the world was he going to say??? He hadn't come up with any answers and nothing in his training had taught him to be political. He was a fighter first, then an investigator, but never a peacemaker. At the moment, he needed to be all of them. There was no way he was going to be able to string bullshit together and it be accepted. It was time for a real plan.

President O'Reilly looked first at the big man beside him. "Charles, you indicated that we might have a even bigger problem than before. I asked you about it and you said that Mr. Curry here, " glancing over at Mike, "knew the case better. That's why I wanted us three to get together because this is critical and I need to stay on top it." He looked at Mike. "Mr. Curry, I know about this dreadful technology and I think any sane person would want to see it eliminated. Bring me up to speed, in your own words."

"First of all please call me Mike, Mr. President."

The president nodded, smiled, and said, "Okay, Mike, and please call me Draven, at least while we're in this room."

Mike smiled. "Okay, Mr. President. Well, sir, as of three weeks ago, we thought that this was all over with, but we had confirmation through NSA sources that someone was holding up the investigation into Senator Lucy Gold."

Draven rolled his index finger horizontally in the air. "Yes, yes, I know this and then someone disappeared."

"Yes, one of the investigators. We know this only by the man that saw him vanish. Nobody else even remembers the guy. ... Anyway, Charlie hears about it, pulls my team in, and we start keeping tabs on Melvin Travis since he was the focal point last time. They break in and kidnap his girlfriend. ... You know, of course, what they want."

"The same thing that they wanted before. The chip."

"Right, it's the key to protecting people from changes in the timeline through the use of time reversion, which Melvin Travis told me that he destroyed. Someone Mr. Travis's wife demanding the chip... Then Melvin himself is kidnapped and we have no idea by whom. Since that time, we've been unable to locate him even though we had numerous trackers on him."

Charles interjected, "We have no idea how, Mr. President. Mike had SIX bugs on the guy."

Mike continued. "Now, this man has disappeared and we've been unable to find him. That's where we stand at present, sir. "

Draven dropped his head and started rubbing his chin. Mike stared at the gray hair atop Draven's head. The thin strands resembled their situation, very thin and fragile. Melvin could be anywhere in the world right now, but according to his file, he had always tackled problems like a rhino charging toward anything that annoyed him. He had always been a loner with no associations.

A man like that was hard to get a feel for: no attachments and no associations except for Margie who was God knows where. There was no telling what he was going to do. As far as his file was concerned, the only time that he'd ever worked with anyone was a few weeks ago.

"Mr. President, Melvin must be being protected by someone," Mike said.

Draven lifted his head and stared at Mike. His blue eyes twinkled. "Oh?"

21

There was silence in the room for a moment and a high-pitched whine pierced the quiet. Both heads turned toward the desk.

A female voice called out, "Mr. President, Vice President Thornburg is here and would like to speak with you."

"Go ahead and send her in, Laura," Draven called out.

Through the mostly white door of the room came Alva Thornburg. Her slim figure stood six-feet tall with firmly lifted B-cup breasts and dark-brown eyes. Her hair, black and straight, flowed to her mid-back. Mike couldn't help but notice her prim walk. He had always admired the waggle of the female anatomy. The butt wiggle was like a masterful, *come hither* to a man. This lady had none of that and he missed it. Mike guessed that having reached the pinnacle of model-dom that she knew *how to* and *how not to* swing those hips as well as when to do each.

It was a strange transition from model to politician. She'd been a Vogue, Modern Woman, and Fashion Magazine model for years as well as many other venues, but as her popularity grew, so did her outspokenness on many debated issues of the world. Her views were popular and she ran for Las Vegas mayor, then governor. The ability to speak candidly had won her favor with the public, but Mike assumed that the fact of her gender was why she was appointed V.P.

She looked at Draven, glanced over at Mike and Charles, and then back again. Her stiff posture exuded calm, but her dark-brown eyes darted questioningly. With a smooth voice, she asked, "Draven, I need an answer to what we discussed this morning?"

"No, I don't think we need to do that, Alva," he said holding his right hand with the 'OK' sign.

With a wave of her right hand, she said, "Alright, Draven." She turned and began walking away.

Draven held a hand up, then said. "Wait, wait. You probably need to be brought up to speed on this anyway."

Alva pivoted on the right heel of her pink stilettos and looked at Draven who motioned her to sit beside him. The next few minutes were spent talking with her about what happened before. The woman reacted well with very few questions. Mike was surprised at her calm, but then again, he guessed that any elected official would sort of get used to being hit from behind. After all, the keys to political survival were adaptability and calm perseverance. After that, the conversation turned to recent events. Again, she asked a few questions, but nothing unexpected.

"That's where we stand, Alva," Draven said.

"This technology is a grave threat to, not just the U.S., but the entire world. Is Mike's team suited to handle the situation?"

"It was Charles's idea as well as mine to keep this as hushed as possible. The last thing we need is for a scare to run through the public and Mike knows the all the details from before."

After glancing at Charles, she looked back at Draven and said, "I suppose that's true." Turning once more, she asked, "So, Mike, you've lost Melvin and still don't know who kidnapped him. What's the plan?"

Oh no! Here it was! It was time for a plan of action. "Well, I have people searching the facility where we think he was at, but so far, we have nothing, but we have fingerprints which we're trying to identify.

We've found Melvin's and Robert Milgrew's thus far. Robert is ex-military, black ops with various agencies, and past federal investigator. He's very smart. We stand little hope of catching up with him. There are three other distinct prints that we're looking into. We found Melvin's cell phone at the scene, but that's it: no papers, no nothing. There weren't even any strange phone numbers."

"So?"

"Robert was leading the investigation into Senator Lucy Gold, but the last notes that we have from his team were the inability to discover a direct link between her and Earth Inc., the company that was doing the research. Shortly after starting his investigation, he resigned his position and went underground.

Up 'til now, there's been no evidence to suggest that he wasn't simply retiring."

"I guess that's been disproven. Either he's after they technology for himself... or..."

"I know the man. He's trying to stop it," Draven said. "Regardless, we have to bring him in."

"You're right, Mr. President," Mike said. "Bringing Robert in is unlikely. He knows how to hid. Our research on Melvin, on the other hand, is that of a *take charge* private investigator who will try to find a solution. The man loves a challenge. A true fighter... but not experienced at hiding... *unless he has help*. Other than these facts, we're still searching for clues and a way to proceed."

"Mr. President," Charles said leaning forward, "we've had a difficult time trying to know even whether we should try and stop the group that has Melvin. ... For all we know, they may be working for the same thing we are."

"*And if they're not?!?!?!?* Maybe these two fighters, as you call them, have teamed up to take matters in their own hands. We need to catch and question them at least!""

Mike nodded. "That's why we're trying to find where they are. During our last attempt to retake Melvin, they must've scattered. "

Alva leaned forward, her eyes were wide and alert. She put a hand to her black hair and swept backward. "Be certain that you keep us posted on the identities of the other three," she said with a gust of air motioning her long pink nails toward Charles.

Draven looked at Mike with his blue eyes that were like the seawater off the coast of the Caribbean. "People," he nodded toward Alva, "this nation, nor the world, can afford for this technology to be in ANY hands. I want to get to the bottom of this and eliminate all equipment, materials, and whatever else. *AM I CRYSTAL CLEAR??? Can I count on all of you?*" he asked as he leaned forward.

A chorus of head nods and *Yes, Sir's* filled the room.

"Very well. Keep me filled in."

They all said their farewells and Draven seated himself behind the desk as everyone exited. Charles exited the door first, then Mike, and lastly Alva. After the door was closed, Alva swatted the back of Mike's right shoulder.

"Hey!" he cried out as he looked back at Alva.

"Sorry, there was a mosquito on your back."

22

Melvin caught Davina's eyes as she glanced at his shriveled body. Both of her cold hands gripped the black steering wheel like a vise. They'd just gotten underway and the only things on his mind were safety and warmth.

"I almost left you," she said.

His body, shivering, his lips, numb, and his flesh feeling icy, sat shivering on the crushed-velvet seat. With his arms, wrapped tightly around his body, grasping for more area, and a full set of chattering teeth, he questioned her, "W ... W ... W ... Why???"

"Because!!! If you had stalled a few seconds more," she held up her left hand with pinched fingers, "JUST A FEW MORE SECONDS," then they could've caught us both. That is something that I cannot permit to happen! Under NO CIRCUMSTANCES!!!"

His teeth chattered more without control. The main thing on his mind was the cold but he couldn't help but wonder if it wouldn't have been such a bad thing to be caught. How was he to know whether they were trying to help or just filled with greed. Although Rob had helped before, there was no guarantee that he was actually trying to do the same this time. What did he really know about him anyway? Not much. Why was he running from Mike anyway?

What about Davina? He only knew her from Rob and the brief meeting that they had had. Who was she really? Rob had said that she came from FBI headquarters, but could he really trust that? They did snatch him away from rescuing, his love, Margie. Rob also asked this hussy about the White House which meant that she was well connected. Maybe too well...

As they drove on, he stared at her warm, dry body. She certainly had creamy, smooth skin and a slim body. The ripples underneath her clothing epitomized bulging muscles. She would have to have the stamina of a horny jackrabbit in springtime because she didn't appear to be winded after their mad trek through the freezing river while even he was huffing a bit. The thought of the near-freezing water sent violent shivers up and down his spine.

As he hunkered beside the door, he asked, "W ... Wh ... Where are we going?"

She glanced in his direction. "We're going to a safe house. Each member of our team outfitted one just in case something like this ever happened."

"W ... Where at?"

Without looking away from the road, she

shook her head and replied, "Yeah, right....
Like I'd really tell you...."

She was snappy, but Melvin guessed it was really none of his business. It was "her" safe house, not his. He was just the unlucky guy who was with her. "So why is Mike Curry such a bad guy?"

"He's not. You see, Mike is just following his orders: a real rule man."

"But he broke those rules last time to help us."

"Yes, he did, but you see Mike no longer answers to the FBI, but to the assistant head of the NSA, Charles Maywear, and that's a whole different continent. Mr. Maywear answers directly to the president and we think they want to weaponize this technology."

"You **think**???"

"Yes, _think_. While you were taking down Earth, Inc., I was trying to get into the administering group of these research labs." She glanced at him and rolled her eyes back to the road. "You have NO IDEA what you tried to break up!" Davina mashed on the brake pedal, then turned left onto a dirt road. The car rolled a few yards more and then stopped. She looked at her passenger who was as huddled to the door and floorboard as possible. "We're here."

"T ... That was quick."

As she jolted the gearshift and turned the key, she said, "Yeah, I don't know what the others chose, but I knew that if anything happened, I wanted to get out of sight as soon as possible."

It was either a brilliant or stupid strategy, only time would prove one right. Either way, they were here now, wherever it was. Melvin shuddered at the thought of getting back out into the cold wind. She didn't even have the decency to turn on the car's heater for the trip.

He was minimally comfortable now and a bit sleepy. The last thing he wanted is to disturb the slight peace he had managed to achieve. "M ... Must we?" he asked slowly. "You could bring me back something to cover up with?"

"I'm not about to let you out of my sight. Besides, this car is going to get ice cold again as soon as I open my door."

As foggy as his mind had become, the words *ice cold*, registered in his brain like a noisy alarm clock. He eased up into his seat. "I suppose. When we count 3, lead the way. ... (big breath looking her way) ... ," He opened the door and looked outside.

There was only a big building mostly composed of gray wood. It was tilted to the right and some of the boards were buckled. The eaves had holes in the shingles, some gaping. He looked back at her.

Davina was walking around the car to the center of the front doors. "Wait, the only thing I see out there is an old barn. Is this your safe house???"

"Yes, yes, yes. C'mon slowpoke." She waved in a come-hither fashion. "We'll be going inside to the back on the right side. After you're in, I'll come back out and move the car inside."

"Okay," Melvin said in a weak, trailing voice. He grabbed the building door-handle and walked it open wide enough for the car. The cold wind sheared right through him like he was an old dishtowel. Every part of his body hurt. It was the kind that echoed through every nerve of the body. He almost wished his stinging flesh would fall off. As he waddled through the barn doors, he saw Davina was anchoring her side open with a rock.

Inside, she passed him and headed straight to the gray door on the right with keys in hand tumbling through the assortment. She found a gold key with a green clover head marketed with an indented black 'SSS' and inserted it. She pushed the door open letting him run inside the black opening. On the right

side, beyond the doorway, was a box on the
wall. She opened the compartment and pushed
up a horizontal black bar. The entranceway and
kitchen lit up.

"Sit, or lay down anywhere, Melvin,"
Davina said. "The heat will start up in a minute.
I'll be back after I pull the car in and lock up."
She looked into the kitchen and saw him ball
up out on a brown kitchen chair.

23

Melvin was already asleep by the time Davina got back inside her safe house. Her secret hideaway had been designed and built into the old barn a number of years ago when she first got into a federal position as her insurance policy... just in case. Being in such a high profile position, she realized that it had always been the way of the higher-ups to blame underlings for anything that became an embarrassment.

However sad it was for any ranking official to scapegoat any of the people they had appointed, whether right or wrong, was unthinkable to her, yet it still happened on a regular basis. Although her position was only assistant FBI director, third level, she'd been directly appointed by President Mathers. She knew that it was only a matter of timing before someone would lay some kind of blame in her. Whether she was dismissed or not, she'd need someplace to lay low until the pressure died down.

In this place, she was away from the public. Not even the land was in her name. She had paid for the five acres in cash. The area used to be a tree farm. Gene Sellers, the former owner, was fifty-five when they met and wanted to sell because of his wife's cancer. He said they had no insurance and needed the money. The price was right at $15,000 so she put in an extra $15,000. She had made it plain the bonus was for his wife's cancer with the stipulation of her anonymity of the entire transaction. Mr. Sellers agreed to the terms with a smile. When they signed the papers, the barn was the only structure on the property, which was infinitely preferable to her.

When Rob selected the bunker, she grinned at the thought of not having to create yet another safe house. She had created so many of them around the world that it was almost second nature, but such a tiring and expensive task.

By the time she got around to building her hideaway here, the barn had become structurally unstable and near crumbling, not that it was great to begin with. As fortune would have it, the stability didn't matter to her. In fact, its inconspicuousness made it more attractive to her. She had the dilapidated structure redone in a matter of weeks. New timbers placed in key areas to shore the structure and build the small apartment.

She smirked as she walked to and through the bedroom door remembering the contractor. He'd thought her insane for wanting to rescue such a rotten building.

She was born in Lake Charles, Louisiana and moved to Baton Rouge at age six. Building her hideaway here seemed natural. She had spent long months working away from home correcting situations that power hungry people had, or were about to, royally fuck up many times before. This time she was working, without authorization, trying to protect a man that represented the only clue that she and her borderline band of traitors had to resolve a hellish situation and protect the reality she knew and loved.

She sighed, then looked around the room and saw her twin bed, closet, and the corner shower. The commode was next to the shower and lavatory on the opposing wall. Not an ideal arrangement, but it was dictated by the building layout, or so the contractor said.

After changing her pants and footwear, she walked to the white on white in-wall drawers, pulled on the second round gold knob exposing the underthings inside. Pushing aside the assortment of colors, she grabbed the black phone underneath, turned it on, and shoved it into her pants pocket.

After washing her hands, she meandered out of the six-by-six bedroom into the living

room and laid down on the tan sofa up against
the outside wall. As her head went back, she
braced the tan throw pillow up against the arm
of the sofa. She blew air straight up through
puckered red lips. "What a day, what a day."
Breathing in, the restful position overcame her
and, for a moment, she was unsure when her
lungs would stop. Eventually, she began
exhaling whispering, "Finally, a moment of
peace."

Feeling warm and cozy was a relief. This
was the first moment she had had to really
relax since the crisis had been re-ignited by
Trace Hooper's death. Much of her time had
been spent trying to separate real evidence
from rumors and bits of false information.
Who knows where the falsehoods were coming
from? That was not her job. Her job was
simple. Get correct information to her boss.

She had a fair amount of dealings with
Rob and had known him long before this crisis.
He was in the military, she, the C.I.A. She
remembered that they had occasional dealings
with each other through his covert ops in the
Middle East War, but they didn't get to be
good friends until his departure from the
military. Having had intermittent talks, he knew
that she had graduated up to the FBI and
contacted her there to explain what she was

really dealing with and swore her to secrecy. Knowing the full truth is what made her decide to live the precarious life as a secret agent. She knew, like he did, that time reversion was dangerous and could alter the very essence of what would normally be deemed reality.

She felt a buzz coming from her pocket. Lifting her eyelids was a struggle, but in the end, they slowly opened. She batted her eyelashes several times as she brought forth the phone from her pocket. The time read 5:13pm. Three hours had gone by which seemed like a few moments. "Hello."

"Hello, Davina, it's Flamecraft." The voice was garbled but there was only one person who had access to call this phone.

"I understand."

"Code: 13 at 10. Can you make it?"

"It will be difficult, but yes."

"Good. See you there."

Davina ended the call with a tap of her index finger and sat up on the tan sofa. Stretching her arms, she stood up whispering, "I've gotta hurry!" She walked into the kitchen where Melvin was out cold sitting upright in the dining chair, arms hanging, head back, and mouth open. She picked up a stack of yellow Post-It's off the kitchen cabinet and the white pen alongside and wrote a note on the top sheet. She tore the paper off, walked up to Melvin, and stuck the thing to his arm.

Walking toward and out of the door, she said, "Good thing this place is soundproof."

24

Davina managed to evade the search parties fine, but the flight to D.C. went by too slowly. Throughout the time, her butt wiggled thinking about the man she left behind even knowing that she would be back soon. Though the *puddle jumper* 737 flight itself was less than two hours, it was only her, and the flight crew. As much as she wanted to talk to any of them, that was a no-go. Idle chit-chat, yes, but nothing beyond that. It was the sad fact of her profession.

In the silence, she hunkered down in her chair. She'd flown many times, but this trip tied her gut in a knot. Something about that phone call had set her nerves on edge. She had gotten phone calls suddenly like that many times before. Why was this one different?

She looked out the tinted car window and told herself it was the fact that she left Melvin alone although she knew that that wasn't what was rattling her. ... bothersome, yes, rattling, no ... The reasoning itself seem to lessen the gripping muscles in her back and that was good enough for her. She sighed.

In D.C., she got into a limousine escorted by men in black and drove away. The ride didn't help her nerves. "The crazy things we tell ourselves," she whispered as the limo's forward motion stopped smoothly at the familiar street corner with a nearly black windowed phone booth on the end. The framing was a wrought iron and it was painted bright gray. She thought it had been somebody's ridiculous idea of making it unobtrusive. Ridiculous! People were going to use the booth regardless. Some were the curious sort, others had a true need, but in these days of wireless electronics the need for phone booths were becoming less every year.

When the limo door opened, a gust of wind whipped into the vehicle. Davina shuddered and pulled her jacket together with icy fingers and zipped it up, then stepped out. She raised her hands to her face and felt of it as the agent closed the door behind her. The booth was only a few feet from her and she began walking toward it. As she entered the bi-fold doorway, she heard the engine rev up and settle into a hum as it drove off. She tuned to the payphone, picked up the receiver, and dialed, '9-0-9", then flicked down the latch twice. "It's, Davina," she said then put the handset back on the latch. The floor began lowering.

It took only two minutes for her to reach the underground hallway. She stepped away from the platform and it began to rise up. She stared a moment before turning toward the chamber.

Inside the walls of cement and flooring of the same came a guard from her right. The rounded-metal fixtures on the roof were wired with surface-mounted conduit and had dim incandescent light bulbs hanging from them. It reminded Davina of the mausoleum that might hold Dracula's coffin. She smirked at the thought. How silly it was to think the most powerful country in the world could bear any resemblance to those silly horror flicks.

As her smile faded, a young male with a boyish face, all of fifteen, walked toward her. He was in a sparkling and uncommon navy uniform that strongly resembled her brother's old cub scout uniform, but without any decorations save two gold buttons on his shoulder.

"Miss," he bellowed on approach.

Davina walked toward the lad. "You don't have to talk so loud, young man. These walls tend to magnify any noise."

"Yes, Ma'am," he said in a lowered voice as he walked near. "I was just making sure you heard me."

Her hands propped on her waist. "Son, do you see anyone else around here?" He muttered and shook his head. "Who else would you be talking to?"

"Nobody, but as for me being a young man... I'm almost twenty-eight."

Davina shook her head. "... just a pup ... Now, ... would you please show me to the meeting room?"

The lad's eyes bulged for a moment. "Certainly, Ma'am. Right this way." He pivoted and extended an arm into the hallway behind him.

The two walked ten-yards down the hallway passing several open doors and a duty station.

The young man ushered her inside and said, "Have a seat. She'll be here any minute." He reached inside the doorway and clicked on three switches. Three rows of long fluorescent lights lit up a large room, complete with a rectangular table, chairs, and monitors in front of six of the other chairs all pointed toward the lone chair at the front.

Davina sat in one of the vacant spots at the front. She folded her arms on the desk and lay her head, face down, onto them. The warmth soothed her face. It was a stark contrast to the icy-cold weather outside. D.C., like Louisiana, had a fairly humid cold but Louisiana's was like wearing a body suit of ice water. Right now, having anything warm to lay her head against, even jacketed arms, was a welcome relief.

The warmth was making her realize how tired she was. Having her eyes closed was relaxing and made everything better. Peaceful. It almost made her forget to push the trusty button deep within her before the meeting. After she did, her eyes closed again. She'd been active for nearly twenty hours now, save the three-hours her eyes were shut in her fortress of solitude, and her body was telling her about it. She could feel her eyes pulse simultaneously with her heartbeat and, strangely, the rhythmic sensation was enjoyable. Her muscles began to ache, yearning for the kind of relaxation that could only come from lying prone on a bed, but she knew that would be a while in coming.

"Davina," a husky female voice said.

She raised her head and saw Alva already sitting on her left. "Yes, Ms. Vice-president?" she asked as she began rubbing the tiny slits that her eyes had become.

"It's time to start the meeting, Dear," Alva said as she eyed her right-hand person. "I wouldn't have sumoned you, but I need your personalized input into this."

"Yes, Ma'am. It's no problem." Looking around the table, she saw that all six monitors were on, but as yet, they had no picture. Alva had already fastened a small microphone to the outside of her navy suit jacket and was handing her one as well. She reached for it with her left hand.

"They should've had you do this already."

"The men might've been just trying to let me sleep."

"I don't care!!! It's their job!!! I have just fifteen minutes for this before I go back to meet Draven!"

Alva had closed the door on her way in and when she sat down, the screens lit up with men of differing shapes and sizes. Mostly they were a mix of Asian, black, and Caucasian. Davina studied them all, trying to memorize each and every face. These meetings were her only opportunity to see them. She had pegged a blonde man and the only woman as leads of two research labs, one in Texas, the other in Wyoming. One man was an oriental named David Golam, the CEO of BioSolutions Laboratory, and the dark black woman as Neva North, research supervisor of Snowder Electronics.

Her research into both companies from her DOJ contact, Barry Simpson, showed that ostensibly each company researched and manufactured weapons-grade technology for the military. Barry told her that it took a lot of favors to obtain the information because they were supposed to be a black-flag operations. Unfortunately, he died a few days after telling her so Davina had assumed that was unlikely timing and retribution for his actions.

Among the others at the table, there was the face of a Larry Stocker who is the Chief Business Advisor for BioSolutions and Steely Mondell, vice-president of Snowder. The other two men always wore white lab coats and she figured were from financial companies. She was pretty sure they were Niles Anderson and Davis Brady, but wasn't exactly certain.

There were no markings on or near the monitors save yellow sticky notes that were affixed to the top with numbers written onto them. Alva never called any of their names during the meetings, just their numbers, and each one was always the same number.

Why Alva allowed her to be there during the meetings, Davina could only guess. Her best idea thus far had been a measure of vanity or security. Alva had a power-glutting streak in her somewhere and she seemed to be always trying to paint a red flag on herself. Davina still remembered the Christmas party when Alva showed up in a white diamond studded dress that probably cost the taxpayers over five-mil.

Alva tumbled a rocker switch embedded in table in front of her with a flick of her long right index finger being careful not to muss the glossed nail. "Hello, All. This is Flamecraft. We have a situation. I've just recently returned from a meeting where I was informed that the man we all know as Melvin Travis no longer has possession of the materials to construct the time sensing circuit. As you know, this is the only reason that we were sparing his life. With Mr. Travis's knowledge about our venture, he is now a liability and must be dealt with accordingly and then there's the other issue that we can deal with by force, if necessary. What say you?"

"Let the other alone," they all said. "It's a non-issue," 3 said.

Alva was slow to react. When she did, it was with a slow nod. "Very well. What about Mr. Travis?"

One, two, and five simultaneously said, "Kill him," but Davina saw 3 and 6 raise their hands. In all the time that she had spent with Alva, she'd never made reference to "another issue". She tilted her head pondering the possibilities and wondering what it was. This was new to her.

She noticed Alva wait a moment for voices to die down, then said, "People, if we kill him outright before he's caught by the authorities, it may look suspicious."

2 said, "Who cares??? The public at large are just dumb idiots that will believe anything we tell them." A chorus of head nods followed.

"Is that what we all think?"

Seeing Melvin's life being cut, Davina looked at Alva saying, "Perhaps we might consider another course. Melvin's direct knowledge isn't the only consideration here. He has a girlfriend named Margie who was in on this too and there's Rob Milgrew too. We need to find these people, find out what knowledge they each may have written down, destroy that too, and then kill them all at once. That way we can frame them in a conspiracy."

"Yes."

"Better plan."

"Let's do that."

"We have to make sure."

"Uh-huh."

Alva's face turned to the monitors. Her lips tightened for a brief moment. "Okay, Group. We're all agreed then. Go back to your work until I contact you next." She twiddled the fingers as she reached for the rocker switch and pushed it off. She looked at Davina to her right, casually saluted, and said, "Thanks, Lady."

Davina still a red face. She knew Alva was in a spin of controlled anger. "Hey, I'm no lady. I'm a jackass like everyone else, but I'm on your side. The only side that makes any sense."

Alva showed her perfectly aligned pearl whites before saying, "Good!!! Now let's get these sons of bitches before all hell breaks loose."

Davina smiled. "Yes, Ma'am. I think I might know where to look."

25

Justin Peters looked back at the cordless phone teetering on the edge of his desk. He'd brushed up against it rushing out to meet Lucy, but figured it wouldn't soon fall to the floor. He was in a rush anyway to deliver his news about Melvin and get answers from his boss. He lurched backward when it started falling and did a tumbling catch jogging his memory about the call he needed to make. Placing the thing to a stable place on the desk caused him to nearly fall.

"Dang it," he said, then jerked the receiver up, dialed, and plowed it into his head.

After two rings, a female answered. "National Security Agency. Assistant Administrator Rachel Jones office."

"Yes, Nancy. This is Justin. Is Rachel in?"

"Oh, yes, Justin. Please hold." With a click, the receiver went silent.

After a few moments, the receiver clicked again with a light female voice saying, "Hello, Justin."

"Hi Rachel. Listen, we need a favor."

"Anything."

"How about an outside lunch?"

"Anyone or anything special?"

"The usual time and place. Today if possible."

"Okay, I'll alert you if it's going to be tomorrow."

"All-righty. Later, Sweets."

"Later."

#

Charles Maywear had been in his office when the call from Rachel came in. "*Why the hell not*," he had said to her invitation. His day was going to the vineyards: smashing, messy, and dirty. Everything he'd touched had gone wrong. It was the perfect day to get away from everything and have a nice relaxing lunch with one of the prettiest women in the office.

Sitting just to the right of his computer screen was a digital clock. 11:51. "*Dang!*" He stared at the clock and thought for a moment. "*Well, crap*! I have the right to leave early once in a while. Maybe my second in command can do the same?" He scooted back, straightened his tie, and stuffed his shirt down his trousers. Good times from past luncheons came to mind. There had been many women in his life, none that lasted. His wife Regina lasted 18 months, but was a disaster. After great dating and a month of honeymoon, things soured. She became mean and spend hearty until bankruptcy and divorce. Any opportunity to forget all that was a treasure. "Nancy, I'm heading out to lunch. Why don't you do the same?"

"Why thank you, Mr. Maywear." Nancy walked up to the rack and grabbed a navy windbreaker from the rack and by the time she looked back, Charles was already headed out.

"Have a good long lunch, Nancy," he said with his back to her.

By the time the elevator arrived at the ground floor, he was all the way to the back of a full load.

Charles waited for the elevator to clear before attempting to walk out. When he was about a foot from the opening, the door started to close again but he stretched his arm out and hit the black plunger before walking on out.

The lobby was mostly tinted windows. The sunlight from a cloudless sky lit up the freshly polished floor with the double-circled eagle seal. He knew it was the season for cold, but the lunch solarium, fifty-feet from the main door, would be warm at least. As he walked to the doors, he pulled his dark-navy dress coat together with one-hand and then stepped on the black-rubber mat. The coldness of the wind stung his face as he trotted to the next building. Unfortunately, his slick dress shoes would not let him run on the cement path between the buildings, lest he fall down and make a spectacle of himself, but he did manage a slow trot.

After he entered the automatic doors of the solarium, he waited until they closed and began gazing from side-to-side looking for either Rachel or an empty table that was clean.

"Are you looking for Rachel," the black man at the cash register asked.

"Why yes!" Charles said. "How did you know???"

"I figured. She said to be on the lookout for you, Mr. Maywear" He pointed to a transparent cubicle at the back left corner.

Charles nodded observing the man's nametag. "Thank you, Chuck." He strutted toward her with a smile and sat in the vacant seat across from her. The bright–orange chair squealed against the floor, but he didn't care. He smiled and said, "These dang chairs do that to me every time. ... It's nice to see a pretty face on a day like today."

Rachel's near-white cheeks turned pink and she turned her head a little. "Awwwwwww... I bet you say that to all the girls. And you a married man..." She shook her head.

"Who me??? Married to my job, you mean. And you have a husband...

"Which I'm happily married to."

"And congratulations for that." He nodded. "There's no way I couldn't make mine work. But even if you are married, that doesn't mean you're dead, right???"

"No, it doesn't. And by the way, women like to look at handsome men. " She winked.

Charles shook his head, then looked at the menu on the ripple-glass table. When he raised back up, he said, "Well, I think that's about enough of that. ... Let's order. I think I'm just going to have a salad."

"Hmmm... that sounds good-make that two."

"Chicken?"

"Yeah..."

Rachel put her hands to the table. "I'll go get 'em."

"Why thank you, ...Ma'am." Charles watched her as she left the cubicle, his eyes fixated on her attractive frame, but something about being alone at the table didn't feel right. It didn't dawn on him what it was until he heard someone come in behind him. "*Damn it*!" He turned around in time to see a rat pull out a chair and sit down. "Hello, Justin. Let's get this over quick. What do you want?"

"Gee, that's a fine greeting you have there, Charles. I can see why you're not in foreign affairs."

"Okay, okay, let's get on with this. *What do you want?*"

"What makes you think that I want something?"

Charles could feel his blood boil and his face along with it. He knew Justin was a mealy-mouth twerp that always meant trouble. "Let's just say *I know your boss.* You're here. *nuff said.* Now, for the last time, what do you want?"

Justin folded his arms on the table. "You are aware, of course, that you have this job due to my bosses influence over certain key members of Congress, correct?"

"Yes, but that has nothing to do with anything. I got this position because I was the most qualified."

"Yes, but you may or may not have gotten the job without the senator's support."

"That may not be true."

"STOP!" Justin held up a hand. "Now the senator needs your support in a matter. I believe that you and the president are involved in a search for Melvin Travis and we want a specific outcome."

I have no idea what you are talking about."

"No matter. You can deny it, but we know it to be true. You owe the senator and she wants Melvin dead."

"Even if I did know *what in the world* you were talking about, that would seem like something highly illegal not to mention unethical."

"Listen, *my boss could squash you like an insect and you know it*!!! You know what kind of power she has. JUST DO IT!!!" Justin pushed back from the table and stood up.

Charles raised his hands.

"Yeah, you can and you must. If you don't want to live, that's a different story altogether. Just get it done, MR. MAYWEAR!"

He was about to walk off when Charles nodded, then called out, "Justin, why are you so loyal to her?"

He paused, then hung his head slightly. "Because she took care of me," he mumbled, turned, and walked off.

Charles leaned over the table and propped his head in his hands. Yes, Lucy Gold could destroy him and anyone else in Washington. She wielded greater power than the president himself. If he didn't obey, he might as well be dead, or worse. He mumbled foul words, then whispered, "I can't do that!?!?!? Why was is this guy so important to Ms. Gold???"

Rachel walked around the corner of the

glass, carrying a tray with two salads on them and several packets of dressing, saying, "I didn't know what dressing you want so I just brought a sample of everything."

He glared at her. "You set me up!!!"

"WHAT???"

"I just had a visit from Justin! Nobody knew I would be here except you!"

Rachel's wide eyes, looked him in the eye, and shook her head. "I have no idea what you're talking about!"

"*You didn't set this up???*"

As she sat down, her red lips formed an almost perfect 'O' as she stressed an enunciated, "Noooooo! ... What in the world did he want?"

"Something incredible. I don't want to talk about it."

"Knowing Senator Gold it's bound to be nefarious."

Charles pulled on one of the salads towards him. "It is, but I'll deal with it. ... Let's eat."

26

Melvin's eyelids flickered open when the jangling noises coming from the door pierced the silence of the tomb which was his refuge, his neck still hunched over from where he had fallen asleep in the dining chair. He moved his hand to rub the throbbing pain as he turned towards the door. It was dumb of him to fall asleep in that horrible position, but at the time, he could push no more.

As a private detective, he had done things like that repeatedly on stakeouts and such. Cops and private dicks both had unpredictable lifestyles. It was terrible to be called away at a moments notice for this, that, and the other thing, but you had to do whatever the case demanded. In the case of private dicks, you had to solve the case or else there was no money.

Solutions were why there was a job in the first place. Policemen, on the other hand, those jerks got paid whether are not they did a good job. The lucky stiffs...! Then again, they had somebody to answer to and he was only responsible to his clients and, if they bugged him too much, he could just drop the] case and tell them where to go, usually someplace not nice.

Still rubbing his neck, Melvin struggled to his feet. By the time that he was standing, Davina was coming in the door. "Hello," he said, peeling the hand written note from his arm.

*

'I'll be back as soon as I
can. Called away to a
meeting. There's food
in the cabinets and
water to drink.
　　　　　-See you
soon, Davina'

*

Melvin looked up from the note. Davina closed the door behind her, let out a heavy sigh, and walked behind Melvin dropping into one of the straight back brown chairs. He carried the note to the table and sat down in front of her.

"How are you?"

"I'm okay, especially for what has been happening recently. Where did you get off to so quickly?"

"I keep a SAT phone hidden in the bedroom. As soon as I got the darn thing and turned it on, it was buzzing with a call."

"I thought phones of any type were ixnay because they could be tracked?"

"Normally, that's true, but this is a SAT phone that I have bouncing off twenty-five random points around the world. As long as I'm not talking for more than thirty-seconds, I don't think anybody is fast enough to get a fix on my position or even close."

"I see. Well, tell me about this trip?"

"It was with the leader of the group and its benefactors. Not much to tell except they want you dead."

Melvin shook his head. "*Oh, great!!!* As if I didn't have enough troubles!" Raising his head, a sudden realization hit him. "You are putting yourself into an awful position, why?"

She grabbed the bag and strolled to the counter so he thought she hadn't heard him. While she emptied the bag of its contents, he repeated himself.

"Why am I helping or why do they want you dead?"

"Both."

She picked up two cans of beans and stuck them in the cabinet. Her normally pale complexion was pink now and in a hushed tone, she replied, "They want you dead because of what you know. Your knowledge has become a liability to them. Secondly, I am helping you because it's the right thing to do." She froze for a brief moment, then said, "I hope you like breakfast burritos?"

He took them from her saying, "Sure."

"I was really hesitant to get involved and no matter if we succeed or fail, my life is over with. If my involvement ever comes to light, and I guarantee you, it will, they will suicide me. We'll all be lucky if we survive."

"Not me. You can keep your secrets, suicide pacts, or whatever. After I get Margie, I'm gone."

"I can appreciate not wanting to get involved. I really can. I didn't want to be involved either. I was leery and hesitant but I want my family to live in a free world that's not contrived and free from radical changes at the whims of the mega-rich-and-powerful people that want to play God."

"You have kids?"

"No. Not even married. I'm 31 and have two nieces. My folks live in Green River, Wyoming."

"What..."

"God I miss them." She wilted and sighed. Hunched over, she re-took her seat at the table and looked up just far enough to gaze into Melvin's eyes. "Melvin, please tell me that they are going to be safe from this anarchy?"

He looked into the blue eyes of the beautiful woman across from him in utter disbelief of her sacrifice for the good of the world. She cared. Misguided as it may be, she cared, and deserved stability and happiness. He was now the reason that she couldn't go back. "We'll do what we can."

Davina put her food back on the table. "I can't eat anymore."

Melvin watched her as she rose up, sniffed, and walked to the sofa. A knot was growing inside his stomach. He folded the wrapper around the half burrito that was left and set it on the table next to hers.

In his life there had only been two sacrificing people. The people from fairy tales... Human beings that despite their wicked tendencies would die before surrendering their good values: Tom and Margie.

Parents didn't count because they made the choice to have kids with full knowledge that youngsters would sometimes be brats. Part of the responsibility of parenthood is to devote oneself to the betterment of their offspring. They didn't ask to be brought into the world and were sure as hell not going to like dealing with the perversity of humankind, but some things you can control, some you can't.

They start as tingles in people's pants. Next, most of the time, there's that moment of "*UH-OH!* What have we done!" and even when there's not, remorse fills the air. Fortunately, he had never made the mistake of spreading his genes. Who would ever *choose* to be born?

Melvin turned to Davina and asked, "*So?* Do you really have a plan for getting out of this?"

She waved an arm grimacing. "Melvin, ...," She sighed. "You may as well face the fact that life as you knew it..." ...a deep breathe... "...is over. ... These bad people will never let us live in peace knowing what we know. That's even "if" we manage to stop them."

Red-faced, he stamped the floor. "That's defeatism talking! I refuse to believe it!" He pounded the table, bellowing, "I don't even know who *THEY* are."

A single tear formed in the inside corner of Davina's right eye. She sniffed. With a shaky voice, she said, "Melvin, this leads very far up."

"I know. The vice president."

"Possibly farther."

"How far?"

"Let's just say that we're dealing with powerful people that can kill us anywhere, anytime."

A cold chill shot down Melvin's spine that cooled his blood. He wondered how far this really did go. They were in a grand canyon of trouble and there was no telling how long the young woman in front of him, who was now doubled-over crying, had been dealing with the stress of being a double-agent.

He watched her trembling in front of him and his gut quaked. How many problems had she dealt with? Without a doubt, she hadn't been trained as a spy and now, at least for a time, her cohorts were all but lost. Melvin put a hand to his cheek and rubbed one side, then the other. He stared a moment more, then with a squeak of his chair, he rose and moved toward her.

Davina sat up immediately, her face, splotchy-red, sniffed, and she said, "I'm sorry."

Melvin continued his approach and wrapped his arms around her. With her head nestled on his shoulder, he said, "Cry all you want to. I'm here." Davina hung her head, sobbed, and from every shudder from her body, Melvin could not help but hold her tighter.

27

"This is Margie again. Well, they have me back in my room. I'm guessing it's a room, not a closet or something so they can keep an eye on me. Although my hands have the chilliness of these metal cuffs, I can feel the cloth material of the flooring. It isn't nearly as awful as the chilly, dampness of tile or concrete would be so I'm at least thankful for that.

I realize what Boss said about wanting to use the time reversion technology for good has merit, but the consequences are too unpredictable. I love Melvin and helped him try to eradicate this technology last time because of trust. I trusted him. I trusted that he would know what was best. He explained how a tiny detail in someone's life could influence their decision making in a big way.

Trust is not something you buy, it is developed between two people over time. You literally depend on someone else's strength of character and knowledge in a given situation. I trust my dear Melvin to know what's best. He's a smart man, but I'll tell you that I don't even think he knows what he wants often times. I believe he wants nothing to do with anyone except me now. It's a great feeling to know that

I'm that important in someone's life. That realization of how much we mean to each other took a long time.

No, love doesn't come quick, but it does come. He's a strange man, a loner, with no place to call home. Our love took over twenty-years to blossom and, truthfully, I still don't think he knows what it means."

#

Margie felt each cold link in the chain that bound her wrists. She didn't find a flaw, only the knobby sections where the wire had been welded together. She'd dealt with lots of chains before from younger years on her grandparents farm for dogs, cattle, goats, and such and knew that the thick metal was not going to give way, but it was always wise to explore all options. She was reminded of Benjamin Franklin who said, "The definition of insanity is doing the same thing over and over and expecting it to come out different." Of course, he also said, "Do not fear mistakes. You will know failure. Continue to reach out."

The sounds of nearby footsteps gave Margie pause.

"Hello again, My Dear," Boss said as he removed her ear covers. When he removed the gag from her mouth, Margie heaved and then started coughing followed by calisthenics with her jaw. "I know. That's not the most comfortable thing in the world."

"That's the truth!"

"Well, it's for the greater good."

"What greater good???"

"I wish I could get you to understand. Our organization doesn't want to hurt anyone except the evildoers in the world."

"Why is my understanding so important to you and just *who are the evildoers*?"

He paused and in her mind, she imagined the figure scratching his head in contemplation. She heard him saying something and asked, "What?"

"Nothing. I'm just getting a chair."

Margie heard the hollow sound of chair rollers on linoleum, then several bumps to the carpeted room followed by a scrunchy-hiss of a leather cushion. "Let's first answer why I want you understand." He cleared his throat of emotion. "You might say that I feel too much. I was a finance exec a few years ago at Lucian Bank in New York. I'd gone to Penn State University, graduated in my mid-20's, got married shortly thereafter. My wife Sara gave birth to our daughter Melissa about a month later."

"It sounds like you had a nice life."

"We did up until two years ago. We were

very happy."

"What happened?"

His voice trembled as he stared saying, "They were supposed to go visit Sara's parents for the weekend out in California. I was supposed to go with them, but the bank was being audited so I had to stay. Anyway, thirty-minutes before they were to board the plane, a terrorist set off a bomb. It destroyed the section where my wife and daughter were. Their bodies were never completely recovered."

"I see," Margie said.

"It's too late to bring them back, because it was never determined who the bombers were. ISIS took responsibility though. ... You see, if I can keep other people from going through death as I have, it'll be worth it to me."

"You mean by eradicating terrorists before they strike?"

"Exactly! It's the same thing for all of us. We are tired of the government system of arming one evil to kill the other. That doesn't work. Saddam Hussein was armed to battle Iran and he subjugated his people, very cruel, and we ended up having to kill him. ... We're tired of all that. Now, we have a way to make the world a better place and save the innocent like my Sara and Jessica."

Margie sat in silence. Her heart ached for him having to be lose his family at a young age. At least she thought he sounded mid-30'ish. It's always an emotional experience to lose a family member, much less two and particularly your own child. My, how he must have suffered... He heart quivered and she felt her guts twisting. These were not people that wanted to harm, but heal, and protect.

This man truly wanted to prevent pain. She quivered.

"You okay?"

"Yeah."

"Okay, as to who the evildoers are, we will form a committee to study behavior patterns of certain people and organizations. There needs to be a consistent track record of humanity crimes. We don't want to use time reversion without strict governing guidelines. ... I don't really know why I'm talking to you so much. I do have the others that I can talk to. I suppose its guilt for having to locked you up this way. I apologize again."

"Listen, you've said that before, now just drop it, okay?"

"Okay, Margie."

"You know, you are a pretty woman, even with your eyes covered."

"Why, thank you."

"You're Welcome. How old are you?"

"32."

"Fantastic! I'm 35 and ugly as the devil himself."

"I bet your wife and daughter didn't think so."

"No they didn't. Lord bless them. I'm sure they went to Heaven."

"How would they feel about what you're doing now?"

"Sara was a *save the world* type. She was big into recycling, supported Green Peace, Rescue The Bears, and, most recently, she was studying on solar energy. I think she would say that the means would justify the outcome as long as it had strong oversight. My daughter was only 5, but as long as we don't harm anyone except the bad people..."

"And the bad people are?"

"Those who would kill, maim, and destroy."

"It certainly looks like your group has thought a lot about this."

"Yes, Ma'am. We don't want to cause any more heartache than necessary. We just want to protect everyone from bad things happening. You know, as a prevention force... We want the world to be a better place."

"I can sort of see that."

"Just sort of? You and Melvin are pretty close..."

"Y-Yes," Margie said. "He is my true love whom I hope one day soon we will re-marry."

"Re-marry?"

"Yes, our first marriage flopped. I suppose we were both too immature. Regardless, we were divorced after a few months, but about a month ago we rekindled our love."

"That's interesting... Tell me, would you save him from pain?"

"'Certainly."

"That's all we're trying to do for the world," he said. "Now, I need to leave you and go check on the others, but I'll be back soon. Think on that while I'm gone."

28

After almost an hour of crying, Davina fell asleep in Melvin's arms. He had known women whose vulnerable natures made men swoon to their sides, but he'd never been one to give in to those wiles. Davina's case was different somehow. Here was a woman who was trying to do good by playing both sides. Having two faces can't be easy.

It reminded him of the infamous Mata Hari who was a spy in the neutral Netherlands during World War I. Her furnishing the Germans with intelligence led to an estimated 50,000 deaths. She was tried and sentenced swiftly without her defense attorney even being able to cross-examine any of the witnesses.

Was that what awaited Davina? She was spying against her own government, but instead of killing, she was trying to save lives. This woman had charm and skill that he'd not seen before. She was doing what she thought was right because the consequences for uncounted people were incalculably bad. Tom saw that and he did what was right too just weeks ago.

Had the death of his only friend, Tom, consumed his mind with rage? His empty heart said it missed friendship. Part of his life had been killed by the same forces that were a threat even now. He never liked humans much to begin with, but was his angered heart now blinding him? Doubting everything in life was normal, but this was something greater. More than sum total of things, was his life over?

"If it is, I'm damn sure going to go out with a bang," he whispered.

He looked down at Davina's wavy auburn hair. There was an occasional tangle, but it was never all at once, like his life. Her creamy, skin was uncommonly soft as he wiped away her tears. The watery mixture dripped from his fingers as his life seems to be taken away from him in small doses. He owed credit to this woman for in recent weeks, it had been her that taught him how to see the beauty of a woman.

It was her protective nature that was saving his life.

He was no longer a loner in the world. He could allow himself to see the good things and it was all because of her. Humans were still miserable, disgusting, treacherous creatures, but like a needle in a haystack, there were rare cases where you find exceptions.

"Wherever you are Margie, I love you," he said.

Davina's body rolled a bit, and her eyelids fluttered. "What did you say, Melvin?"

Melvin looked down into her soft browns realizing what he had said so near to the woman who was protecting him. She might have taken offense to, what sounded like, his putting his love ahead of her cause, so he replied, "Nothing. I was just mumbling something to myself."

The beauty of life made him more convinced now than ever that he didn't want anyone messing with the balance of life. He'd be morally damned by his own conscience if he did not help her try to eradicate this technology from existence. If she could risk her life to save his miserable hide, then there was hope. This was more far reaching that he had ever thought possible. What would happen if they were to use this technology to bring somebody back to life? Greedy bastards! Would that person even have a soul? Tom knew the dangers well enough and laid this problem from hell at his feet knowing that he would take care of it. He had to.

It would be like Frankenstein's monster all over again. It went against the forces of nature. Although the devils could possibly bring his parents back to life, it would change the person he was right now. He didn't want to change. He wanted his anger. He wanted his pain. If parents could take back the children that were discovered at any age to have detrimental illnesses such as muscular dystrophy, bi-polar, cancer, etc., then we wouldn't have people like the great physicist Stephen Hawking and many other greats.

He was living a nightmare and regardless if he quit now or stayed the course, his life, Davina's, and whoever else would never be the same, particularly those fighting against the technology of time reversion.

After a while, Melvin fell asleep with his arms full of womanhood. He had no idea how long he slept, but when he woke it was from a kiss on the cheek. Davina's soft lips gave him a warm fuzzy feeling as if it was a reassurance that everything was going to be alright.

"Wake up sleepyhead," she called out.

Melvin, still in a sitting position, stretched his arms and yawned. "What time is it?"

She rubbed his right arm down to his hand and clutched it while gently pulling himself to a sitting position. "Nearly 8:30 a.m."

"That cold really must have tired you out."

"I guess it did although I hate to think of myself as a weakling like that."

"Not at all, you're only human after all."

Melvin grimaced at the dirty word. To be compared to something that he despised being was one thing, but "human"? Those people were the worst things in the world. He was human, but he certainly didn't like the comparison. With a nod, he simply got up and said, "Probably so."

Humans. Humph! He sneered as he got up. What in the world was it coming to when he was changing into a flawed human? Other than Margie, Tom, and Davina, he had no use for anybody and he certainly didn't trust this new woman much. She just seemed a nice, likable girl who was under a lot of stress, but there was something more that he could not deny feeling. It was a feeling that he didn't like. It went against his philosophy of trusting only himself. She hadn't earned that level of respect yet. He didn't know when or if she would ever do enough to earn that.

"What would you like for breakfast," she asked standing in front of the stove.

As he admired her big perky breasts, he noticed that she had changed her clothes and asked, "I see you changed. By any chance, would you have a change of clothes for me?"

"No, afraid not. Why don't you come and sit at the table. We can have the rest of our breakfast burritos."

"Okay, they are only a few hours old anyway. I'm sorry for teasing by asking you what you wanted."

They both sat down, Margie gave thanks to the Lord for the meal, then they both ate. Melvin patted his belly afterward. The meal barely stopped the growl of his stomach so he began chugging the glass of water that Davina had set beside him. He looked up at her as her last bite was shoved inside. The lost look was gone from her face. She had been recharged by last night's meltdown. Of that, he was glad, but not wanting to say something is never the same as not having to. "You know, we can't hide here indefinitely. They will find us eventually. Anyway, why can't we use the same route that you got to your meeting?"

Davina shook her head. "No. That was a one-off. It was my escape route and once I used it, it closed, and it was difficult to get back here." She reached for the clear glass in front of her saying, "You're right about our need to get out of the here though, but beyond protecting us both, I'm not sure of what to do."

"Well, surely you have some tentative plans of what to do if you were ever relegated to this hideout?'

After emptying the glass of its contents,

she replied, "Yes, my escape hatch, but we can't use THAT again! ...just like I said and it didn't include protecting a man whom everybody wants to kill or use anyway!"

Melvin thrust his head back and paused. She was right about that, but ... instead of hammering a rusty nail, he decided to work around the subject. "Well, we're safe that's for sure but we only have a brief reprieve. It won't be long before they start going door to door and even though we're hidden, your car is not. They'll tear this building down hunting for us."

"I know this. At the time that I built this place, I never even considered trying to hide from satellite thermal scans. Not from here anyway." She motioned a hand toward him. "We're lucky they haven't spotted us yet. Of course, in this shack, they may think we're game animals."

"True. That won't last long though. We can't run anywhere without at least some kind of plan," she said with a lurch, throwing her napkin onto the table. "We can't afford to amble about and hope something comes up. Well, ... You're from the FBI, right?"

"Right."

"Well, who do you know well and work with besides the bad guys?"

There's Rob, of course."

"Who is missing..."

"Yes. Then there's Simone Carter and Rachel Jones who are both assistant FBI directors, although, I would not look for help from either of them."

"Why not?"

Davina looked up at the ceiling and huffed. When she looked down at Melvin, she said, "Because Simone a real turncoat B who is out for herself and Rachel is a backstabbing hussy who is on Senator Gold's payroll. She gets away with a lot of crap because men think with their penis's."

Melvin groaned, then shook his head. "Who else?"

"Well, there is Mark White. He is the deputy FBI director. I don't know much about him except that he kind of has a reputation as a ladies man. I wouldn't hold that against him, but neither would I trust him simply because he is an unknown factor and I don't know exactly which way he will go. He may turn us in." Davina put her hand on top of his. "Melvin, this is getting us nowhere."

After thinking a moment, Melvin slipped his hand out from under hers. He was irritated, but trying not to let it show. Her touching hands probably meant he was doing a *not so good* job. Still, the answer was in her, she just didn't realize it, so he said, "You're right. We are going about this the wrong way. It's my fault for not phrasing my question correctly. Who in Washington could you trust?"

Davina put her hand back on top of his and said, "Well, at the moment there is only one man who I could trust."

"Who???"

"Charles Maywear."

Melvin leaned back in his chair whistling. "Isn't he the director of the NSA???"

"Not quite. More like assistant and a very good friend. He and Rob were in the Middle East war together. I got to know him pretty well through Rob. When Charles came to the NSA, I was already there. We worked together for many years, but when the opportunity came up in the FBI as an assistant, I jumped on it because it was a lot more money."

"Do you think he would help us?"

Davina grabbed his hand and rubbed. "Yeah, maybe. He certainly wouldn't give us away."

She was obviously a *toucher*, but was she making a pass at him? He was certainly not going for it. "Listen, I'm a married man."

She pulled her hand away. "I know. I wouldn't ask you to do anything..."

He shook his head. "I won't. Margie

means everything to me."

"I know," she whispered with a bob of the head.

He nodded. "Alright then. How do we go to Mr. Maywear?"

29

"Melvin, it'll be difficult to reach Charles. I'm sure that by now they've found and identified my prints all over the bunker we were using."

Melvin put his hand atop hers and gazed into her eyes. He was determined to charge forward and play detective as he was used to doing for so many years. He caressed her hand with gentle fingers, saying, "Davina, there needs to be a way for us to get to D.C."

She cast her eyes downward. "Ordinarily I'd just call our pilot, Zac, but I saw on the news during the flight back that he was killed."

"I thought since your group split that you didn't know where anybody was? ... And just how did you manage a flight???"

"First of all, it's by far easier for me to sneak around by myself."

"As an investigator, I totally understand that."

"Second of all, the route I took to get out of here was my safety valve, one use only. Only reason I used it, was to gather intel. Third, you may know some of what I'm talking about, but I doubt all. Zac was my ace in the hole with many private airstrips." She buried her face in her hands.

An inaudible thud made Melvin's heart quiver. This small, scattered group needed one for skills and support it seemed. "How???"

"Driven off the road and shot," she said while twin tears ran down her cheeks.

Melvin reached up from the table and wiped them up, one at a time. "I'm so sorry."

Empty eyes stared up at him. "Well, is there any other way from here, wherever *here* is?"

"We're on the far north side of Baton Rouge. ...Above St. Francisville... and "yes"... Zac has air strip is about 20 miles northwest of here. ... The biggest question will be, can we get there unseen..."

"Well, we sure can't go on foot... Not 20 miles..."

Margie looked at him, her eyes flashing. *"Yeah, get real! That's a no-can-do."*

"Well, then need we'll need a car, can we drive yours?"

"Since they know who I am by now, I'd say that we'd be spotted by satellite as soon as we pulled out. ... Hmmm, speaking of satellite..." Davina sprang toward the living room.

What was she doing? She obviously had an idea, but what? Melvin followed her and saw the tablet computer that she was pulling from behind the sofa. She unplugged the white charging cord and put the thing in front of her.

"This thing is untraceable. I can patch into satellites and see if there are any *cars that we can borrow* and where the search teams are. I really should've been monitoring things all along. ... I'm such a fool."

Melvin grabbed her shoulders and started massaging. He didn't really know why. It was a compulsion that he knew that he would later regret. Humans were a despicable lot! No one helped, they all rode the coat tails of others until the time came when they could smash people and get ahead. Only, they failed to realize that it was all a sick game of humanity beating itself up for thirty pieces of silver.

Davina's head lurched backward, still staring at the tablet. "I've got it! They seem to be concentrating their search on the south and southwest sides right along the stream we walked up. Of course, that could change, but for them all the air support and troops are in that area and there looks to be a army-green truck by the side of the road just a mile-and-a-half up the road. It may belong to a hunter and we'll just have to hope it runs, but at least its a target."

Melvin stopped his shoulder rub and sat

down beside her. "I can definitely hotwire it. Being a P.I. gives a lot of unlawful training." He laughed. She flashed him a smile and rose from her seat with a twinkle in her eye. It warmed his innards, even though he didn't want them to be so. It was annoying to wither and show pathetic emotion again. WHOA! WHAT WAS HE DOING?!?!? He slapped his face.

Davina's head snapped up. "*What was THAT for*???"

Melvin looked at his hand. He heard her question and his mind was trying to think of something, anything to qualify his reaction, but she not experienced the gut jolt that he had. He could feel air hitting his round eyeballs and all he manage to utter was, "Huh?"

"Wake up, Dear. Where are you?"

"Never mind," he said in a crescendo. "It's not important. Just bad, bad thoughts."

"Well, wake up!" She pushed the tablet in front of him and pointed at the screen, saying, "Looky here. There's the truck."

Melvin cocked his head. "Where's the hunters you spoke about?"

She grabbed his shoulder. "Who cares? The truck's there and you know those hunters. They're go after defenseless animals with bazookas and camoflauge. Humph! Some sport, huh?"

He smirked with agreement and surprise that a woman thought as he did about anything. He gave a quick nod. "Exactly right! And why not take a chance especially if one is all you have because it looks like it was the only usable vehicle of any type for at least 10-miles."

"You ready, Popper?"

"Yep. Ready and anxious to kick butt."

She scraped the tablet off the table. "Ready, Sweetie."

There it was again. Melvin's gut was saying things that he'd rather not hear. As he got up, he asked, "Can we take that thing?"

"You bet your bippy."

What's a bippy? As he bolted towards the door, he decided he'd rather not ask.

30

When Melvin saw the garage door swing open, he squinched his eyes together from the brightness. He liked the sunlight, but much preferred his serene back yard with its many shade trees. Davina motioned for him to come out from the covering. It was now or never, he thought as he gulped air. He really didn't want to step outside, but wanted to find Margie and get lost in one another. He was tired of this mess. When would everyone just leave him alone?

Davina was walking about four-feet in front of him waggling her rear-end. All women were built with hips that swayed and hypnotized. They couldn't help it. It was just the way they were. At the moment though, it was very distracting because Margie was his love, yet somehow, promiscuity filled his loins. He didn't have time for adulterous struggles. Every person had them, but there were far more pressing matters. So far, they had no plan except for getting to this Maywear guy and he was trying to think beyond the struggles of getting there.

How did they get involved in trying to find people that he only knew from the news?

He wanted to get help, yes, but they might have to hogtie this guy to get him to listen. He knew only two people that he trusted and that was Margie and himself. Were they leaping into the lion's mouth?

He knew that Davina had knowledge which he lacked about D.C., its policies, and the ways to reach people without getting caught. It bothered him. He'd rarely been outside Louisiana and his only trips of any sort came while he was still in school. It bugged him, but he still considered himself adaptable. He'd always been self-sufficient until Tom dumped a mess in his lap three weeks ago and thereafter he'd been committed to helping. His longtime friend died on him still leaving a mess that he'd needed others to help resolve. It sounded like a circus show, but yet it happened.

A good life with a woman was not what he was expecting to find when Tom had nearly kidnapped him, but now he was looking forward to it with Margie. He'd learned, the hard way, that he needed to depend on others to achieve objectives. It went against his better judgment, but it was a good lesson. He'd depended on Margie and it got him through. Through the ordeal, they'd found love again and had the happiest last three weeks of his life.

In front of him, Davina's rear kept wagging. Although it was a good sight, he trotted to her side. He didn't need her eye-candy. He turned to her and asked, "Do you think this Charles will help us?"

Davina turned to him, saying, "I think so, but no one can guarantee the actions of anyone, but I think so. Besides, I have another safe house in D.C. anyway."

He shivered. "Damn, Girl! You have backups for your backups!"

"I learned from the best."

"Who?"

"Rob."

"That sounds like him," Melvin said with a smile.

She chortled. "Well, when you're playing on both sides, you have to have to plan for every contingency."

He shrugged again. "I suppose so. Just how long have you been doing this?"

She put a hand to her to face. "Hmm... I guess I learned about time reversion about three years ago. It was then that I started working my way into their organization. It was hard to earn their trust at first but by being Benedict Arnold to everything I ever knew, I earned Alva's trust and I'm seen as a close advisor now. "

"You've certainly been doing this longer than I have. ..."

"Well, it's not my service that's important, what I'm working toward is. When I first was approached about this, I found the whole thing ridiculous. No one can reverse time, I thought, but it was true."

"Who approached you?"

"I'd rather not say at this point."

"Why," Melvin asked in a high-pitch.

"To protect them and you." She twisted toward him. "Look! I'm in a precarious position here. I hope you can understand and overlook some stuff."

"Like what???"

"Like the need for secrecy."

"What about the public's right to know," Melvin asked with raised hands.

"If the public really knew a lot of things, they'd have a heart attack." Davina stopped, turned toward Melvin, and said, "Look! There so much crap that I've seen... There are some who would never believe it and, those that would, they'd make it a million times worse by scaring everybody else out of nine-lives. The publics right to know, yeah right. This is just one of the ludicrous things that I've dealt with. ... And I don't even know all of it. Our government is so compartmentalized that different branches are so loosely associated with the mainstream that no one knows what they do." She turned and started walking again around a sharp curve.

"Gee, sorry I asked."

She slowed, looked at him and said, "I apologize. My frustration at not being able to correct bad situations gets the better of me sometimes." Before he could answer, she pointed and said, "Look! There it is." "Come on!"

Sixty-yards from them was an army-green GMC by the side of the road and Davina was already running towards it. Melvin was a pace or two behind her partially watching her backside as it wiggled while mentally cursing himself.

"Margie, Margie, Margie," he whispered. He jolted to a stop at the driver's side door where Davina was already fidgeting with the lock. Moments later, there was a click followed by her opening of the door and pressing the *unlock* button. Melvin grabbed the door handle. Its coldness made him recoil his arm. It was a reminder that on this temperate breezy day, it was still February, a frozen wasteland of little opportunity. He had only the flame in his heart to warm him.

"*GET IN,*" Davina called out.

The urgency of her voice startled hi and he grabbed the cold metal again, this time opening the door. Davina had already started the truck by the time he sat in the cloth seat. As he pulled the door closed, she drove off, immediately making a U-turn on the narrow road, but not succeeding. "*Damn,*" she said backing the truck up. When it moved again, it spun tires and slung gravel one way as it sped down the blacktop.

Melvin's stomach was telling him that it'd been a while since breakfast. "I hope there's food at this airport?"

She glanced at him. "Certainly. You should realize by now that I'm always prepared."

"*Yeah, I guess,*" he said softly. What awaited them on their quest was still a mystery and he knew it invited great danger. There was a knot in the pit of stomach. He was out of his league. His skills as a P.I. were handy, but at the moment, he had to rely on her. He didn't like it but he had no choice. "I wish Rob was here. I like that guy. I hope he's okay," Melvin said with a sigh.

31

Margie's muscles tensed when she heard someone's footsteps near her. Other than distant shouting a while after Boss had left, there had been silence for quite a while.

She was getting tired of the darkness of her blindfold, but was not about to threaten her freedom by trying to remove it. The less she knew, the better. But, Boss certainly was intent on getting through to her that their group was trying to do a good thing. Why?

If bad people could have their actions vanquished, that might be bad, but it could be a good thing as well. It probably wouldn't affect good peoples lives. If people knew that the price for crime was the forfeiture of every action they've ever done, it could lower the crime rate immensely.

In her blackness she heard muffled footsteps outside the door, which she presumed was closed. Her muscles tensed when she heard the knob turn and the door, which she knew to be hollow by the shallow sound of fingernails dragging across, open.

"Hello again, My Dear," Boss said. "I need to talk some more. Are you game?"

Davina nodded and her gag was

removed. "Sure, why not," she said. "Why is it so important to you that I understand?"

"Because I need you to know that I'm not some sort of monster. I'm a decent, law-abiding human being that's trying to help the world."

"That may be so," she said, "but here you are."

"Exactly. I detest that a good-looking woman thinks I'm your common criminal."

"Well, talking's better than just sitting here." She heard the creak of a weighted chair and turned herself toward the noise.

"Have you been thinking about what we're doing here?"

"Yes," she answered, "but has my Melvin turned up?"

"No. He hasn't. ... You know, he never had to be an orphan?"

"What do you mean?"

"I mean if we were to have accomplished our objective back then, we could've helped his parents."

"From obesity??? That's basically what killed them."

"What about intervention counseling? I mean if we know what's going to happen..."

'Well, I suppose that's true," Margie whispered. By the time she realized that she had spoken soft, she'd lowered her head and Boss was already asking if it was shame. "No," she said knowing the truth.

"I wouldn't blame you if you did feel that way. After all, it's not something one ordinarily thinks is possible. ... If we could have saved his parents, then we could've also saved yours. I know they were killed by a terrorist bombing. What would you do to have the two that gave you birth back?"

Margie shuddered.

She could hear Boss chuckle. "Of course, if one or both things happened, you and Melvin would possibly not have gotten married or even met but think about how much happier you'd be. ... There's so much negativity that we all carry with us every day. Imagine if that were gone?"

After moments had passed, Margie realized her thoughts were humming audibly and her head was doing something. She stopped making sounds and opened her mouth to try and speak, but her heart couldn't grasp the thought of not being with her love. She knew the logic, but was unable to break loose of her emotions. "Nooo," she yelled. "I can't lose him!"

"Maybe you would be together. There's no way of knowing what would happen. Still, there is a theory of *Eddies Of The Heart* which implies which says that no matter what transpires in life that the heart knows better what we want and need than the brain. Parents love their children no matter even if they murder someone, right?"

"I suppose so."

"Then no matter what changes time will have, they will always love their kids and according to this theory, if you love someone in one reality, then you love them in all realities. I will always love my wife, no matter what."

Davina thought a moment. She wanted to help this man find peace. "You could save your wife too."

"Well, for me, I decided a long time ago not to try to go back and rekindle my life as it was only to help others find their peace. For you, they say that "Love is eternal," and you could find your perfect like. It's a possibility, but when we can maneuver time like this, who knows what can happen?"

Margie didn't really hear Boss, but knew his words were rattling around in her mind somewhere. *Happy,* was the one word that kept buzzing in her mind. With the exception of the last several weeks, Melvin hadn't really ever been happy. From years ago, she remembered his smiles on their wedding day, but not beyond. He'd never talked much and she never did understand his liking that darkened house of his. Maybe it was the deaths of his parents at a young age that led to his negative outlook? "I suppose he would be a lot happier if things in his life had turned out different."

"I know that you love him."

"Yes, I do," she whispered. Her head plunged after she spoke. Knowing the difference between daylight and dark was one thing, but right now her emotions were convoluted. She loved Melvin, but knew he was distant. Even in these last three weeks of love, fun, and harmony, there was a part of him that she couldn't reach.

"I know you love him, but would you do anything for his happiness even if it meant losing him?"

Margie tried clearing her throat of her heart. Trembling, she tried swallowing the lump in her throat, only it wouldn't go away. This was an inroad. She knew her tension wouldn't go away until she made some sort of decision about her life. She knew that trying to change the past was somehow wrong, but to allow someone to have daily struggles with a dark past when there was a power to help them was wrong too, yet both seemed right too. She put her palms together, mumbled in whispers so Boss couldn't hear her prayer.

Her words seemed to go on for long minutes while Boss talked on as she didn't want what she was sure would come next. *Dear Lord, should love be so hard? Why should I have to choose between two right choices for both of our lives? Do I give up in order to receive? Is this even about me or him? Please heal my heart. Amen.*

"I don't blame your indecision, but know that you're a lovely woman both inside and out. I've watched from afar a long time planning how to catch you without harm to either one of you. As careful as Melvin Travis is, that wasn't easy. I bet you didn't know that he set up security traps? He loves you, but is really insecure. You could help him so very much. I want to help both of you to be happy. Please help him by helping us!"

Margie put one hand to her face and the other to her chest to try and ease their aches. Her heart was sending electric shocks to her body. The tingles shot from her toes to her head and back again. Was she going to do right or wrong? And which was which?

"Not only you," Boss said, "think of the billions of people this could help!"

Underneath the blinding hood, Margie's face began to soak in her tears. She knew that fear was ruling her and she had to get past it. If Melvin could be happier, even without her, she was willing to sacrifice anything. His happiness meant everything. "Please," she said. "Please help, My Love."

After a few scuffling noises, her blinder was removed.

32

After getting Melvin into her cinder block underground hideaway in D.C., Davina ran to meet her boss. Living a triple-headed life had not been easy. Allegiance to her job and country was easy. Playing goodie-two-shoes in a rogue, quasi-anti-government operation was harder, but pretending to be a malevolent person fighting for world dominance was the hardest.

Now, she was caught playing nursemaid to a guy that, due to his critical mistake, might've blown everything that she'd worked for. She'd been only somewhat recharged at her hideaway and, of course, she had to fly the Learjet, which stiffened her neck and back all over again. Now, here she sat, in the backroom of an abandoned building with a sagging ceiling, peeling wallpaper, and a dust covered, tarnished tile floor waiting to meet someone that may never come. Her only contact was a darkened figure that stayed away from her vision with a garbled voice.

Now here she sat on a dirty bench. At least her long coat protected her from the filth on the filth. The soiled feeling made her feel that this was all wrong, but this was her chosen path and, damn it, she was good at it. She knew her cause was just, yet she was in the ruins of humanity seeking help from a dark figure who seemed to have answers before she thought of questions.

Stabs at her scalp made her poke fingers underneath her white panama hat to scratch and afterward set the oversized thing on the edge of the bench.

When the dark figure had first approached her, she was skeptical and didn't want to be involved, but the more the dark figure talked, the more it seemed they had to be in the government. Whoever it was had too much intricate knowledge. They knew how government worked: slow, compartmental, and inefficient. They also knew she was working with Nancy and Petry in the Middle East war running covert ops.

That was never put to any reports. She was never there, officially. One man gave her the order to go there to help those operations go smoothly and that was Rob. Nothing on Earth could ever crack him. So, there was no choice.

So, like many times before, she became a spy for whatever government black ops this was. *Save the world* was the only unspoken motto of hers in this venture.

She looked around the room and saw nothing but dirt and dust layered over everything. Who was she to do this? It was always the job that dictated her life. Some parts of it she enjoyed. It got her adrenaline pumping most of the time in a good way, but with Melvin in the picture, most of the time she was scared of fouling up. He was obstinate, but the man was hurting and she could feel his pain, not only about his girl, but life itself.

She slid her feet on the floor and the created streaks. Maybe she was fondly dreaming that her arbitrary hero would show up and tell her how to proceed. Maybe the dirt and filth of the room and the disgusting nature of mixing it up with deplorables was making her pipe dream. But time and again, she came back here to meet her darkness like, whomever it was, said to do.

She didn't know how, but each time the figure always knew when she was in this place, staying far off, in the shadows, concealed by clothing, hats, or behind walls. Each time, whomever it was, always provided whatever she needed. This time she was after information and resources.

She reached to rub her neck when she heard a garbled voice.

"I know your situation. Why are you

here?"

Davina looked and saw a shadowed figure in the darkness standing twenty-feet away. Her hands fell to her lap. "I need help."

"Obviously. What kind?"

"I have Melvin Travis tucked away, but, I'm not sure where to go from here. I have no idea where Rob, or any of the team I was working with is, and I have no information resources to go to except Charles Maywear."

"Stop!!! DO NOT go to him!"

"Why?!?!? He's a very good friend."

"Don't count on that! He's being manipulated by forces even he doesn't know."

"If that's really true... then I don't know how to proceed."

"There's bound to be someone you can turn to?"

She shivered. The situation needed a resolution and she didn't have one. "In all of Washington, Charles is the only that I thought that I could count on. If I can't, I have no idea who I can. You know, I'm a field girl, usually undercover. I don't make a lot friends in D.C."

"Aw, to heck with this," the voice said as a hand jumped behind its head.

"What?!?!?"

The shadow approached her. "Davina, I'm sorry for this cloak and dagger routine."

Davina knew the un-garbled voice and, as the shadow closed on her, her notions were realized. "Rob!!!"

33

"Yes, it's me," Rob said holding the voice collar.

Davina jumped up and threw her arms around his with a sigh. "I thought you might be dead," she screeched though her mind said otherwise. Rob was her boss and her mind shouted at her that the hug was wrong. She lurched backward. He was supposed to be the one that had been working AGAINST the government. She pulled fists in front of her and was poised on her toes before she realized what she was doing. But, ... wait! This was the man that had helped her through the years. She relaxed her combat-readiness for an instant, only to raise her fists again.

She looked into his dim face and saw only the same steadiness that he'd always had. "But wait, if you've been... You were trying to destroy this technology... You told me that you left your position when you saw the corruption." Rob glanced down, then looked deep into her eyes. His brown eyes softened as he put the back of his hand to her cheek for an instant.

"I'm sorry, Davina. Just know that I follow orders too. I'm working for and against the government, but both are against time reversion."

She relaxed her stance, reached for his arm, and rubbed. Orders she understood. "I feel for you, Friend, but I'm desperate for help." He put a hand atop hers.

"I know. That's why I exposed myself. We need Charles Maywear's help, but if you go to him, even with your past relationship, I'm afraid he'd turn you in."

"What about you?"

"I have an entirely different relationship with him. He'd listen to me without risk."

"Are you sure, Old Friend?"

Rob turned her hand over. "I'm sure. I know things about him that he can't afford to let anyone know, plus we were great friends at Carson Long."

"The military institute?"

"Yes. We were roomies until we graduated."

"And you think that gives you immunity?"

"That and the secrets."

What secrets, she asked herself, but decided against asking him. Instead, the rev of pent up anxiety was shooting through her legs like the crack of a rifle shot. In an instant, they became vessels of energy that needed excising as demons. She began a brisk and accentuated walk, hands clasped behind her back. She still didn't know what to do about anything.

"What's wrong?"

"You talking to him still leaves me without a plan," she said as she grinded her feet against the dirt-laden floor.

"Well, ... for the moment Charles is the key. You see, I work for Gen. Mark Landry from the Joint Chiefs Of Staff. The military has been investigating this whole thing for a while."

Davina stopped, turned, and asked, "Why, and why isn't the FBI investigating? That's their job."

"Well, you remember Mike Curry?"

She huffed with a nod and said, "Of course,"

"That guy is working for Charles..."

Davina gasped through an open mouth. It seemed that everyone that she'd been close to through the years had a hidden agenda. Propping herself on the wall behind her, she began to wonder how she was going to protect Melvin. Bringing him to D.C. might not have be the best thing for everyone.

"... but he doesn't realize that he's just a pawn. In fact, neither of them do. ... That's what I was about to tell everyone when the FBI showed up."

Davina didn't know what to say.

"I know," Rob said, "it's a lot to take in all at once."

She nodded. "Yeah, like really. Who in the hell is Charles reporting to?"

"For your own protection, I can't tell you. I can only warn you to stay out of sight, both you and Melvin. Keep your SAT phone on you. Don't trust anybody!"

After pausing a moment, Davina thrust her hands forward. "By any chance, do you mean Vice President Alva Thornburg?"

"Holy crap, YES!!! How do you know???"

"I'm spying in her organization. It's taken me a year to earn her trust as an expert."

Rob's glaring told her what she needed to know. "Operatives are everywhere. Be careful who even sees you. Be aware though, we think Alva might not be the end."

"Will do, Boss." Davina grabbed her hat, snugged it on, and turned toward the door. She took a step, stopped, and said, "Thank you, Rob, I don't know what I would've done without you." She turned only to stare at an empty room.

34

Melvin's eyes flickered open as he moaned at the thought of having to get out of bed. Thoughts of Margie being scared, alone, and pain ridden pervaded his dreams. "I dare not think like that," he whispered to himself.

Not able to put his dreams aside, he jerked himself to a sitting position, rubbed his eyes and grinded out, "Argh! Wake up, Melvin! Wake Up!" Ending in a low-volume scream, his own words resonating in his ears.

He felt the warmth of frustration fill his face and wiped at it with both hands, only it wouldn't go away. "Come on, Melvin..." Outstretching arms in front of him, he took in a deep breath which turned into a giant yawn. "Shit! I've got to snap out of this!" With a thrash of his head, he jerked himself to his feet.

When he did, the rush of a winter draft whisked over his skin and, for a moment, he stood still. The shock dissipated quickly. He grabbed the underwear and pants off the floor and sat back on the bed. Once he stepped into the leg holes, he looked down at his shriveled groin. "Poor, Willie. You've been through the ringer, haven't you?" He stood, pulled and fastened the pants. As he was putting his shirt on, he heard Davina call out to him.

Stomping as he walked, Melvin charged into the five-foot square that was the living room. The whites of Davina's eyes were at full peak, but he didn't care. Margie needed his help and he was determined not to fail her so nothing else meant anything.

"What was the name of the guy who you were going to see???"

Davina slouched a bit and her eyes resumed their normal appearance. "Charles Maywear, but that's no longer a good idea."

"Why not???"

"Well, it's just not. I was told to back off and lay low." She plopped down in the green easy chair that was against the wall and put her face into open hands and wiped.

"Where's this dude at?"

"Currently he has an office in D.C."

"WHERE?!?!?"

"The pentagon."

"I'm going to see him. You want to come along?"

"WAIT!" Davina jumped up. "You can't!" She reached to grab his right arm, but he was weary of any more restraint and quickly pulled away. Davina grabbed for the other arm, but he backpedaled. "You don't understand! That place is impenetrable. The powers that be want you six-feet under the ground and, preferably, scorched and dismembered."

"What powers???"

She shoved him into the sofa. "How about the fucking Vice-President Of The United States?!?!?!"

Melvin remembered. He didn't care. He didn't like sitting on his hands ever! "Listen, my life has been turned upside-down ever since this shit-storm happened!"

Davina stood. "Look, Melvin," she opened her hands in front of her as she stood, "He may not be the end of this thing. There may be more..."
Melvin's nergetic legs from seconds ago became weak and felt himself stumble. It was slight and he didn't think she noticed, but he knew. The implications were vast and he didn't want to think of everyone who could be involved. He dropped himself back onto the sofa and his head went to rest on the back of the cream sofa. "WHOA!"

Davina threw her arms up. "Yeah!" She sat down beside Melvin and took his hand into both of hers. "I'm sorry that I had to tell you that."

He appreciated her candor and thanked her for the truth, then said, "We have to get all of these people some kind of way." He rubbed his chin. "So when does this Maywear goes home, can we get this guy then?"

"There's really no way."

"Where's this guy live?"

"Why? Will you rush out for an ambush?"

"Something like that."

She put her hands atop his, squeezed, and with glaring eyes said, "You're crazy! Didn't you hear me? Alva Thornburg wants you dead or don't you know what that means?"

He wriggled his hands free from hers. "Oh, I know what it means, but some things are more important."

She pulled her hands away and stuck them in the air. "You fool! You're handsome, but you're also a damned idiot!"

"I may be a fool, but I have to rescue Margie," Melvin said before he realized her compliment. "You think I'm handsome, huh?"

She pulled away. "Ummm... Yes, I do."

It was a sweet comment and he took a deep breathe before saying, "I appreciate it and were I not already involved, I might think longer about it. Right now though I need to hurry back to my girl. You see, it's as much for me as it is for her."

Leaning forward, she began rubbing his hand. "Why as..."

"Stop it! I'm not talking about this anymore! Either you help me or I'll go it on my own!"

"Where would you look?"

"Listen, woman, I'm a P.I.! I can find where to look. Your help would just make it easier. *I'm not the sitting type.*"

Melvin saw Davina put her head in hand. He decided to let her have her moment rather than disrupt her thinking. She was trying to stall and he knew it. Did she not want to help him rescue Margie? She'd been trying to hide stuff. He couldn't care less about her politics, her secrets, or her agenda. He had one motive. She could be a drunken prom queen as long as she helped. He knew that for him to take charge was not in her plans for sure. "You have thirty-seconds to decide. After that, I'm headed out."

She eased her hand out and shook his. "I'll help and protect you, but first I need to use the restroom."

He didn't want to let her go, but had little choice. Feeling the throb of his temples, he slapped his hands together and said, "Go! I'm leaving in one-minute!"

35

Looking up form the floorboard of a car might've be unusual, but Melvin didn't mind being unobtrusive. It was exactly what he wanted anyway, to be unnoticed by everyone except Davina. They were safer that way.

Davina had given him a hat and painted his face with makeup before they'd left. It wasn't a lot, just enough for him to be not so instantly recognizable. However much he didn't think it necessary, she'd insisted, although the drive to the abandoned Flen building was short. Looking up at her, he couldn't see that there was a beautiful woman under the wrappings of that brown hat, but he knew it was her all the same.

Being cloaked and inconspicuous by choice was one thing. This was something else. He'd hunted folks to see what they were doing, but he'd never been the hunted until three weeks ago. These people wanted him dead, worse yet, they wanted him cut up into tiny pieces along with everyone he ever knew. It reminded him an episode of *Espionage* where they always wanted Agent Dan Fowler dead.

Like each episode where Dan needed help, he did too. He neither wanted to depend on Davina nor could do anything about it because he couldn't do it without her. As able-bodied as he was, he needed her. They were on the verge of *talking* to Mr. Maywear and unraveling this nightmare. His cohort had told him that the best time to catch the guy was at the Flen in late afternoon. "That's where he stays sometimes to get away from everything," she had said. "It may take days, but we may get lucky."

Her explanation was reasonable, yet her sudden willingness to help kept dinging in his head. This was the same girl who ruthlessly defended her position to keep hidden. Was she switching tactics to fight the war? If she were setting him up to get caught by people who would for surely kill him it would be out of character. She'd been protecting him and there was no reason to believe she wouldn't continue doing so. He knew, the same as her, that this was a game of such high stakes. Her betrayal, this far in, would be so contrary to that notion that he decided not to upset her by questioning his only current ally. He only hoped he wasn't fooling himself...

As much as he despised it, he trusted Davina, but only to a certain extent. Tom and Margie were the only exceptions. Tom was that friend who you meet once in a lifetime that you just clicked together as one person. Margie was his life-mate. She'd proven that she was as like-minded as he was. Distrustful of humanity and open hearted to him. That was good. He stared at his smooth-skinned compatriot trusting, perhaps, that he had found his second Good woman. A brrown-eyed beauty...

"What," she asked without looking down at him.

"Nothing. Were I not involved, I'd tell you that you were pretty."

"What does being involved have to do with beauty, wherever it's found?"

She was right, but to say so, just felt wrong. "Nothing, ... I guess. ... "

"Well, thank you, anyway." She ducked low to the seat hindering his clear view of the darkened sky and put a finger to her lips.

Melvin heard the hum of a well-tuned engine as it grew near and parked nearby. After the engine went off, he heard the deep thud of the car door, followed by the beeps of an alarm activating.

Davina laid down on the seat. "We're in luck. He's here. ... We'll give him a few minutes to settle in," she whispered.

With a simple nod, Melvin looked away from Davina's face. She was beautiful with the body of a high-class model and could've done whatever she wanted. She laid on the seat with her face pointed toward him. His downcast eyes were now at her feet. What a nightmare, he thought as he closed his eyes. He'd taken a deep breath, but not exhaled, when he heard her whisper.

"Penny for your thoughts?"

Exhaling first, he said, "They aren't worth it. Nobody's is, but I sure wish Tom was here so I could ask him, *Why me?* I sure never wanted any of this."

Her blue eyes batted. "I know what you mean. ... Well, I've heard of Tom, but what was he like?"

"What initially attracted me to him is he had respect. He cherished..."

"What do you mean, respect?"

"People will tell you that they respect this or that, but when it interferes with them and what they want.... Give you an example: Suppose you have a friend who has a house. You work for the city and they want to put a road through your friend's house. Imminent domain, right?"

"Right."

"WRONG! Respect! The friend may do everything right according to the laws and everything else and according to the law, he's still going to lose his house. Not right! Most..."

"What..."

"Wait! Most people, after all is said and done, will protect their damn job!"

"What could he do? He needs that job?"

"Be trampled on too, if necessary. People that really have respect will do whatever is necessary. Respect means loyalty and doing whatever is necessary."

"That's idealistic dreaming," she grunted.

"Right is right, no matter what! ... And that's why I want no part of humanity!" He sneered. "Greed for self..."

She sat up. "Be that as it may, Tom helped everyone get into this mess, now it's up to us to try and fix it."

"*I thought we DID*! Now it seems like everybody in the world wants to me either dead or kidnapped." Melvin crawled up from the floorboard, moaning with every move. "I'm not as young as I used to be."

"Ready, Hot Rod?"

Why was she so anxious when she didn't want to do this anyway? While pondering the possibility of a trap, he said, "Yeah," then grabbed the door handle.

36

Melvin stepped only where Davina did through the glass doorway as Tom had taught him. He sensed danger and, why not, Mr. Maywear was a government official. There was no telling what booby traps his NSA training had laid. He was also probably stealing money from the taxpayers just like every other person sucking on the official tit. Human greed had no end.

The insides of the building reflected the outside, vacant, rundown. It appeared as though the place used to be a merchant storefront. Several floor-attached tables were here, no chairs, and a service counter about ten feet long, all covered with many layers of thick dust. The lighting fixtures the same... The linoleum flooring had many divots, scrapes, and jagged holes as well as dust layers but the layers were broken up by separations which had to be made by Charles feet.

Melvin followed Davina through the shadowy room into a hallway where she opened a door. The lighting within silhouetted her frame as she entered the room. He decided to remain behind her after she entered.

"Davina! I haven't seen you in a while,"

Charles said from behind a large table.

"Well, I'm not sure you'll like me after this."

Melvin stepped out. "Hello there. I'm here to settle a few things." He inched forward and heard Charles stammer.

Recovering, Charles snapped his arm up with pointed finger. "YOU!" He jerked his arm down and darted towards the open door behind him.

Melvin started to sprint after him, but stopped when a dark figure entered the room from the rear door. It was Rob! and his face was like a rock. With quick footsteps he blocked Charles shuffling feet behind the table.

Charles spun around and locked eyes with Melvin. With a blood curdling, scraggly voice he asked, "What do you want, Melvin?"

Melvin could feel Charles heated anger but didn't care. "It's like this, I don't like running from everyone and fearing for my life."

Rob pushed the only chair in the room to Charles backside. "Sit down and listen, Boss."

"Boss???" Melvin felt flush with what??? Was it anger or surprise? "Why Boss?!?"

Davina charged forward and stiff-armed the table with a thud. "I'd like the answer to that too, Rob? I mean I thought this was the very thing we were fighting?"

Rob closed his eyes and hung his head for an instant. Looking up, his eyes locked onto Davina's. "It was. The situation became so very complex. Boss, do you want to explain to them?"

Charles scowled. "Go ahead. You're doing okay."

"It did start out as Charles and I fighting time reversion, in fact, it was him who came to me with evidence that showed there were others researching the damnable stuff." Rob started rubbing Charles' shoulders. "When they started pressuring my friend here to support their research, he cut ties with me, officially, to bring them out."

Melvin snapped, "So he's a double-agent!"

Charles jumped up. "Yes I am! ... Just don't ever forget that I'm a good guy," he said before sitting back down. "Public service is not about service, it's about love of country. ... It *should be* anyway." He leaned back. "I've found out that people who I've admired were only about what their job could do for them, greedy son's of bitch's."

Melvin felt the warmth of camaraderie. Charles was now realizing the truth that he'd always known. "The truth sucks doesn't it," he asked.

"Yes. Outside of the people in this room, there is no one that I can trust," Charles said.

"That's exactly what I mean," said Melvin with curdled laughter. Out of place, yes, but he just couldn't help himself.

Rob kicked a heel with a contorted face. "Lay off, Melvin! We all agree with you, but the real question is how much can Charles help us."

"People, I really don't know how I can help you."

Davina stepped forward. "You must be able to do something?"

"Other than suicide, I don't see how."

"Everyone's human, Pal," said Melvin, "and everyone has weaknesses."

Charles portly body turned toward Davina with a pointed finger. "Keep this animal away from me. I'm supposed to kill him anyway!"

"Bring it on, Fatso!"

Davina grabbed Charles by his suit coat. "What did you say??? Who told you to do that???"

A wide-eyed Charles answered, "Senator Gold."

"Herself?!?"

"No. Justin told me."

"WOW!"

"What's *WOW*, Davina," Rob asked.

"I was in a meeting just this morning in which I convinced VP Thornburg and that council to delay in killing Melvin."

37

Charles unseated himself. "So do we have another player?"

Davina shifted her weight, saying, "Somehow, I don't think so."

Melvin's anger was boiling up. None of this was about the one issue he really cared about. He pounded the table with a fist.

Charles put hands over his ears. "SON! You don't need to do that!"

"Damn it, I want to know where Margie is! That's all in the hell I care about! Save the world, later, save Margie, NOW!"

Rob threw his hand up. "Wait, wait, wait... By dealing with things in order, we hope to help everyone or don't you care?"

"I care, but I need to see about her first and I think this guy," he pointed at Charles, "knows where she is." A red-faced Charles looking at him told him all he needed to know. He'd stomp fatso into the ground if that's what it took.

"Look, Melvin," Charles said, "you *really* might not want to know what's become of her."

"Maybe not, but my first priority is to her. Now, are you going to tell me willingly or are you going to suffer a while and then tell me?

Rob waved at Charles. "You might as tell him, Boss. We'll help him as much as we can, otherwise they'll kill him and we need his knowledge and experience."

Charles shook his head. "Well then, your girl was carted off to East Texas near some podunk community called Bon Weir. The... "

"*Oh great!* More travel."

"The area is thick with trees and underbrush and the building is only guarded by one man on the outside and three inside. It's easy to spot on a satellite."

"Let's go then!"

"As much as you need help," Charles said, "we can't go with you. Like you, we have our duties and priorities."

"Damn it! I can't go in there alone!"

"Yeah. Boss! That's just crazy to let him go it alone!"

Charles glanced at Rob. "We just can't help you, Melvin. We have to deal with things here."

Davina stepped forward. "Well, I don't answer to either of you and I'm going with him. It may be the only way he comes out alive, but I want to ask *just what in the hell is wrong with you*, Charles?"

He stood up. "I like you, Davina, but I'm following my orders on this."

"Whose orders???"

"I can't say."

"*Yeah, yeah, yeah,*" Melvin sneered. As he turned, he waved a hand in disgust. In an instant, he walked towards the door and heard footsteps grind the dirt on the floor behind him. Although he saw through a red uncaring haze, once he reached the next room, he turned. He only saw a glimpse of Davina's auburn hair before she plowed into the back of him, her 36-inch bosom acted as a bumper between them, while her lips nudged into his nose. "I guess it's just the two of us then."

"You got that right. We may get killed, but we're gonna try."

Davina looked over her shoulder and turned back with droopy cheeks and eyes. She was disappointed and who could blame her. To expect more from friends was normal. To be disappointed by helpers was the thick of humanity and it made Melvin's gut churn. He expected this, but not her.

38

Melvin sat in a muted silence on the plane trip to Lake Charles, Louisiana. Contemplating the absurd ethics of Charles was making him reevaluate his involvement in this mess. Was he committed to this or not? Humanity was disloyal and without an ounce of morality. It felt like Rob wanted to help him, but Charles was pulling rank. What was the reason? "Boss" was probably the answer, but it seemed their experiences together were more important. In a right world, lives were more important than anything.

It had been Margie and her love that pulled him through hell and thereby awakened his heart. Her life was more important than anything. By rescuing her, he could destroy their leverage on him. He would be the king of his domain again. It's not as if he hadn't been King of his world anyway, he just didn't like anybody to have leverage over him.

The educated morons... They were stupid enough to mess around with time reversion anyway. That's the height of humanities greed. It was just like people to leap and then look and realize the question they should've asked in the first place: *Should we?*

Davina had landed somewhere where they could switch planes but Melvin didn't ask any questions or even speak during the switch. He didn't care why they were switching. He just cared about getting there. The new plane ended up being a single engine Cessna that they boarded and soon they were on their way again.

She had tried to engage him in conversation, but he was too focused on rescuing his love. He was so near. His mind realized that she was well on the way to being secure in his arms, but his nerves were afire. His insides were trembling with anticipation of a reunion, one that would steady him. He saw the dingy fields outside his side window and felt his heart sink.

They were lifeless, slumbering until the next season. Was it an omen? An audible gasp escaped him before he even thought.

"What did you say?"

Melvin decided to remain quiet no matter what Davina wanted and said, "Nothing." It was short and simple, yes, but he'd rather hold on to his anxiety for reasons that perplexed him. Maybe it was to save energy for what was to come.

The landing was as gentle as one could be and after signing off with the tower, Davina pulled in by the hanger. "Okay, you go ahead."

The icy February wind seemed to cut straight through Melvin's jacket like it wasn't even there sending shivers down his back. He walked around, looking at the still-twirling prop, misshapen like humanity, and saw Davina talking to a long-sleeve overalled man with a black beard. What they were saying was unimportant. She was getting him to his love.

After their talk, Davina and the man switched places and he moved the plane behind the building. The office was a short distance away. Melvin rubbed his eyes and by the time he looked up, he saw Davina, waving, fifteen-feet away. It was time to go.

He burst into a near run catching up to her. He bumped her into her side sliding to a stop.

"Okay, Anxious. Be my guest," Davina said backing up with a waive of her hand.

When Melvin put his hand to the car door, the icy wind washed over his face. He hesitated for a moment thinking about the possibilities of both good and bad. He longed for a reunion with Margie, but what if she was dead? Could he live with that? What if she had been tortured and was in Great Pain? His mind could conjure up worse things, of that, he was sure, but in an instant he decided to not dwell on those bad things for one more instant and surveyed the auto.

It was a black sedan. A dark-haired man in a bright blue tracksuit was leaning against it just behind the front tire with an expressionless face. Melon sneered.

"What's the matter?"

Melvin just shook his head. "What is it with you people and black sedan's?"

"What do you mean?"

"I mean all of the cars that you use are black sedan's. Down here nobody drives a black anything. It's too dang hot!"

"Well, it is just the government's idea. I don't know why they do it. Just bear with it and get in the vehicle."

Although he knew that they would be as inconspicuous as a bright red apple on an orange tree, he jumped in the black monster on the passenger side. Perhaps, given the winter months that they wouldn't stick out too bad. This dreary winter had gone on far too long. The cold was melting into his soul and Margie was the only answer.

"Ready to go, Sport," Davina asked of him like they were going to the store to pick up a keg of beer for a football party.

"Hell, yes! That's what we're here for, isn't it??" he responded in irritated anger at her belittlement of the moment.

After an awkward stare, Davina's eyes softened. She looked at his outstretched hand on the seat and spoke with a soft voice. "We'll find her, Melvin."

The hurt look on her face made him regret his gut twist and he stared at her until they drove away. Although he spoke firm, nausea like that of a young kid having to speak in public for the first time was twirling in his stomach. He was going to witness his future. He put a hand to his face and felt the weeping of his eyes. Maybe she wouldn't notice his emotions, but he felt she could. She said nothing.

39

Senator Gold was resting in her office after an intelligence committee briefing. She'd been there all of three minutes when Charles walked in. It was no surprise however, she'd sent for him on the basis of corroborating information from the hearing. Smiling, she said with a chipper voice, "Charles! Come in. Close the door and sit down!"

"Don't mind if I do," he said knowing the cordialness was a command. She took her seat as well after closing the door.

She gazed at his entire body, stiffened, and then looked straight into his eyes. "I only have one question for you."

"Yes?"

She laid both palms flat on the desk and leaned forward. "Where *in the hell is Matthew Craps?*"

"I have no idea. I mean he was a great worker for Senator Longview who was investigating you, then he just disappeared."

Thee senator snapped her fingers at him and jumped to her feet. "Enough with the bullshit... Just tell me where he is."

"That's what I'm trying to tell you. I don't..."

"Hogwash! I don't believe as a high ranking NSA agent that you aren't intimately familiar safe houses and what they're doing!.!.!."

"I'm not! If I knew where Mr. Craps was, I'd tell you."

"You don't where HE is, but do you know where safe houses are?"

"No. I don't."

"Can you get access to that information?"

"I seriously doubt it."

"I want him dead!"

"I know, but I have no knowledge of such things and for me to nose around in that mess would jeopardize my position. I just can't help."

"Is Melvin dead yet???"

""Not that I know of."

"I want that man's blood spattered from here to Africa."

"Why?"

"That little imp fouled me up before and I'm not going to let him do it to me ever again.! Do you know where he is?"

"Last I heard, he was headed to save his ex-wife Margie."

"You told him where she was?""

"I had to. He managed to catch up with me."

"Okay," she smiled.

""Why is that good?"

The senator retook her seat and picked up the phone, dialed, and said, "They're headed your way." She hung the receiver up.

"Who was that?"

"I have scouts on the lookout where Margie is."

"Smart thinking."

"I was never a scout, but I like to be prepared."

Charles smiled and clapped his hands repeatedly. "Way to go, Boss Lady. I'm assuming you'll want Melvin killed, right?"

"No. There's another plan."

"But? You just said you wanted him dead?"

"Yes, that was assuming we couldn't catch him." She waved her hand. "Anybody can be USED! After that, 'he will die a horrible death and probably not even understand why."

"*Hmmmmm....*"

40

During the long ride to Bon Weir, Melvin's gut kept flip-flopping. It was sick and disgusting. It felt like a hurricane inside him bashing his long ago dinner and its digestive acids against his stomach walls. Nausea forced him to put the window down, rise up, and put his face in the icy wind trying to relieve the jitters that was shooting through every nook and crevice in his body. It dissected and shredded his muscles bringing with it a searing pain. Davina asked what he was doing but he wasn't comfortable with the truth. Fear was his truth and it was disgusting. It was not something he was used to. His business as a P.I. was easy and unless a gun was pointed to his head, which was rare, there was no reason not to be a brave adult. This feeling was different and it scared him but he didn't want anyone to know his truth. "Just feeling the wind," he said.

For a while she was patient, but that ran out. She shouted, "Cut it out! It's freezing in here!" He pulled himself inside and warmed up. After mere moments, his tension built again and he put the window down again to resume his dog position and let his face flap in the wind.

Davina would get irritated and yell at him again, but what the hell. This was probably typical for her to try to save the world by charging into hostile territory. His woman had been kidnapped by these bastards to control him and he despised the feeling of being in someone's pocket. Davina was at least helping him go into the lion's den. Few people had helped him in life, least of all, someone he barely knew. That took a great woman... or he was a hell of a man. He didn't believe that of course but it made a tug at the corners of his mouth.

"We're nearing the GPS coordinates."

Melvin retook his seat and put the window up. His head was cold, but the cold wind circulating on his face had helped him steady him. The pungent aroma of fear that was all around and inside him had dissipated. His guts were still quivering, but he'd always heard that a bit of tension kept a person alert. It'd always been true for him, but the stakes had never been this high or this personal. He hoped he was up to the challenge. When he tried to swallow, the lump in his throat didn't go down easy, but thereafter he managed to ask, "Where at?"

"It's about 3 miles ahead. If the security is

like satellite views and Charles indicated, this should be easy."

Melvin rubbed his hands together. He wasn't sure if it was if it was the cold or anxiety that made him do it but his heart was pounding. "Let's hope so," he said.

"I know you're nervous, but try not to be," Davina said looking at him with soft eyes. "We'll get her."

Melvin turned his bottom lip inward and bit down. It was no use trying to hide it so he said it aloud, "I'm afraid of what we'll find."

"A certain amount of fear is good. It gets the adrenaline flowing, but you don't want it to overwhelm you. Then you make mistakes."

He heard her words, understood their meaning, but also knew he was *riding too high* on emotion. There was nothing he could do about his situation except try to deal with it. "I've been nervous before, but never like this."

"I'm sure you'll do okay," Davina said pulling the car over. "I have faith."

Melvin saw pine trees every 3-feet mixed with underbrush and decaying pine straw on the ground. It was a rustic area that made him feel uneasy. Up ahead one-hundred-feet was an intersection with a dirt road barren of traffic. Margie was down there, he could feel it in his gut. The road they were to traverse had three-inch ruts and a ridge of center grass that appeared to be surviving by sheer will under the rough treatment of all manner of vehicles. It would be rough walking, but doable.

Davina opened the center console and pulled out an eight-inch knife in a brown leather scabbard and tucked it in the small of her back underneath her blouse. She looked up, smiled. She said, "Standard issue in all field vehicles..." She put a finger to her lips and got out. He eased himself out of the door, then gently pushed near closed. A gentle breeze brushed the cold, humid air onto his skin and caused chill bumps to rise. He shuddered, but saw Davina was nearing the front of the hood. He tucked himself in behind her wondering how far would they have to walk, thought about asking, but his knot-tied gut made him decide against it.

A few cowbirds were chirping in the near leafless elm trees making them appear black in large areas. The trees were pitted against gray stratus clouds that made the day seem wanton of death. Melvin walked in the left rut behind Davina who was making long strides. She was advancing her lead on him, so he quickened his pace. The footing was unsteady in the ruts forcing him to be cautious where his feet landed as any guards might notice footprints in the ruts. He respected Charles but only one sentry was unlikely. They might find a deceptive Fort Knox.

Up ahead on the right sat a vanilla trailer with brown trim with Davina looking towards it. The clumping of trees in the area thinned out around the rustic, dirt-laden, trailer and the yard looked to be one big gray and red dirt pile with an occasional patch of weeds dotting the area.

Davina stooped behind a Maple tree and motioned with her hand. Moving beyond her, he saw a burly man coming from behind the trailer. He had a rifle strapped to his shoulder and a black moustache. Atop his head was a hunter-green baseball cap. He walked in front of the trailer, looked around, and began walking toward the back corner. Melvin looked at Davina who raised one hand following behind the guy. *Here we go*, Melvin thought. She pulled the knife from her back, caught up to him, and grabbed his left shoulder and shoved the knife underneath his ribs, tip-point up. The burly man crumpled to the ground without even a gasp.

Davina grabbed the body underneath the shoulders and started dragging it. Melvin stared at her efforts and with a giant leap from behind the trees, rushed to her side. She scowled, but

let him wrestle one arm away from her, and
they tugged the big man's body behind a group
of trees.

"*You don't listen very well, do you?*" she
scrawled with a quiet voice.

"Nope."

41

David T. Cogley's specialty was locating. Whether it was people or things, he could always do the job better than anyone else and every now and then he'd have to prove he was the best. He'd located jewelry, people, buildings, and even a lost mine from 150-years ago. All successfully found. He'd done work for the police, attorneys, and millionaires. Now, at 43-years-of-age, if he didn't know someone well, he charged $5,000 just for a consultation.

He had just found the lost brother of Sama Jang-Ju, originally from Iraq, who hadn't been seen or heard from in 12 years. He had chosen to vanish into New York City because of being repeatedly embarrassed by his family, or so he thought. David didn't care about the reasons, just the payday.

He'd just arrived at his office, from the back entrance, and began organizing bills to pay when a thought crossed his mind. He buzzed Liz on the intercom. "Would you come in here a minute and bring any messages, Liz?"

From the speaker, a soft voice said, "Yes sir. I'll be right in."

Moments later, in walks the long-blonde-haired beauty he'd hired 8-years ago for her blue eyes and sexy body, 38-20-34. He hands her a stack of papers. "Pay these."

"Yes, sir." She took the bills with one hand and sets some papers down in from of him, bending over enough to reveal the top of her boobs as she often did. Her red lips curled up showing off a beautiful smile. He knew the sexy show was for his benefit, but her beauty and assets were why he hired her to begin with. She knew it too because he'd told her and thereby she flaunted her body for him. She could've sued, but where else could she be a secretary making a quarter-mil each year with a golden parachute agreement of 5-mil. Besides, her contract had a non-disclosure-agreement attached to it.

She wiggled her breasts and derriere as she rose up, saying, "There's three inquiry's. One from someone named Geoffrey Jump. The other two are from repeaters: Sally Olson and Paul Watley."

Her wiggles appealed to his groin and made him wanton of someone to bed besides his fist. Being able to buy sexy women had advantages, just more time for it would be better. He'd been married only once for 6-months and vowed to never repeat the mistake, only to embrace desire.

David ran an open hand from his bald

head down over his face. "Let's size these leads up on the desk shall we? I'll throw Mr. Jump to the side." He rifles through the papers and hands a page back to her. "Let's turn Sally and Paul down on the desk and mix them up." He moves the pages blindly. "Now, Ms. Liz, pick one."

"Having fun with this, are we?"

He Smiled and said, "Sure. Why not?"

Liz leans over the desk once more and turns over one of the pages. David's burly arm tilted the page up. "Ah, Sally," David said with a smile. "Thank you, Liz, that'll be all for now, put the other two in my leads basket. I'll outline the invoice for Jang-Ju in a bit."

"Okay, Mr. Head Honcho," she says as she grabs the pages then turns her back and wiggles out.

After she closes the door, David exhales through pursed lips and says, "I don't know how she uses her body like that, but damn, she's sexy." He swallowed hard. "Alright, Ms. Olson, what've you got for me?" After reading the brief caption, he picked up the white phone receiver from the desk and pushed one of the buttons on the phone. "Liz, get Sally on the line."

42

Melvin saw Davina's eyes flare and her face turned redder than it already was. He didn't care though. She needed the help and it was up to him to give it.

She grabbed the .38 pistol from the guy's holster, checked it good, and got to her feet. After a glance at the trailer, she turned back towards him. Her eyes fixated on his with a cold, steel-like gaze and whispered, "This time, do exactly as I say, *don't think*, **just do**, or you'll kill us both. *Stay **behind** me*." He nodded and watched her backside as she walked toward the front door knowing that if she needed help, he'd be there whether or not she wanted it.

When she got to the steps, she took great care with each of the three black-metal steps up to the door. On the top platform, she eased her ear to the door and stayed there. Long minutes passed before she moved. After knocking on the door, she backed away. When the door opened, the barrel of a pistol peeped out then a man crept out behind it. He began to turn and look behind the door when Davina grasped the gun in her hand, holding it chest-level, and yelled, "FREEZE!"

The man turned toward Davina and let

his .38 swing on one finger. She side-stepped to keep the man to her front.

"Grab that by the barrel slowly and toss it over here by my feet. You can tell your buddies in there to throw their weapons out too or..."

"'Stop!!! Stop!!!" screamed a woman as she rushed outside, urging her companion down the steps as she hurried down after him. "This isn't necessary!"

"Throw a..."

Melvin recognized Margie instantly and, without a breath, stepped out from behind Davina. "MARGIE," he shouted.

She spun toward him and burst into a sprint. "MELVIN!"

"NOOOOOOO!!!" Davina yelled looking back.

Melvin stood in place ogling the woman he loved. Every cell in his body yearned to rush into her arms and place his lips to hers but caution and the trust he had vested in Davina through their time together tempered his actions. As Margie started dashing towards him, another man's head emerged from the doorway.

"Come on out," Davina shouted still aiming the gun. The man did as told with hands open and above his head. "And you can tell everyone else to come out too and I know how many of you there are."

The second man turned back toward the door and hollered, "Come on out Axel." As he made his way down the steps, a third man stepped out and made his way to the ground.

When they were all out of the trailer, she motioned behind her. "Okay, Melvin, come on."

He felt his heart jumpstart his legs and pull him into a sprint toward Margie. As soon as he did, he saw her start running as well. When they met, he took her into his arms and pressed his lips to hers, caressing her body. "I missed you," he said as his aching body moved from one area of her body to others. He didn't know if he was testing her reality or wanting to feel her inside him. The only thing he was certain of was that he had what he wanted and the rest of the world could go to hell.

The world seemed to be right again. Feeling her warm, supportive flesh was all he needed. In these long hours of her being away nothing had seemed right. He'd been a husk waiting to be filled again and now she was here. All seemed right.

He took a step back to look at her. From her auburn hair to the tennis shoes on her feet, she was a thing of beauty. "Where did you get the clothes from?"

"From them." she waved an arm behind her. "Meet Axel, Matt, and Mark."

The three started to wave until Davina waived them off by twitching the gun.

Melvin took a step back. "You know these guys?

Margie stepped forward. "Well, no... not at first... but the more we talked, the more I realized that this technology was not so perverse. It can..."

"*It can what??? Destroy the world?!?!?! Destroy reality?!?!?!*"

"NO, NO, NO!!! It's not like that!"

He covered his ears. He couldn't hear anymore. Not Margie too! He felt his knees lose their strength and sink to the loose gray dirt below him. He felt Margie rush to cradle his arm. He tried to push at her side ending up putting his arm alongside hers. "You know what this technology is! We fought it together, talked about it. We tried to destroy it!"

Margie caressed his face with one hand. "I didn't really understand what we were doing or the power of what we were trying to stop. Once I understood, I joined them."

"This isn't good Melvin," Davina said. "We need to get out of here."

"*Give me a second,*" Melvin said, his voice wavering.

" I mean now!"

43

Melvin looked at Davina. He had trusted her to get him to Margie, but now everything was all messed up. He gazed at Margie while Davina shouted in his ear, but somehow everything was muffled. Somehow everything was happening slow and fast all at once. In front of him was Margie, his love, who he had sacrificed and longed for, who was pulling his arm saying *stay* and to his side was Davina who was busy throwing their guns deep into the foliage. He could only stare at Margie with fumbling steps backwards. He could see the hurt in her eyes and wiped at his own eyes. This was the person he most trusted... The person he loved.

Davina shoved Margie back, grabbed his hand, and shouted, **"We've got to GO!"**

He started to shove Davina, but couldn't. He didn't know why but he turned and began running with her, but when he did, he saw the hurt look in Margie's eyes and he thought he saw tear drops form in her eyes as she knelt to the ground. Did she do that in remorse or separation? Davina pulled him around and said something he didn't understand while running toward their car.

They seemed to arrive there in an instant and she shoved him inside before climbing in herself. What was happening? Why did Margie run back to them instead of to him?

He heard the engine rev up and his mind said, *NO.* He reached for the steering wheel, he heard her shout and she pushed him away.

"We've got to get out of here as quick as possible. *I'm sorry, Melvin.* She's working for them now."

"I DON'T EVEN KNOW WHO THE FUCK *THEM* IS!!!!!!!!" He turned toward her and propped a bent leg on the seat as she started the car and pulled onto the road.

"We've gotta get outta here!"

Melvin grabbed both sides of his head. Nothing was going good. "No, no, no."

"What's no?"

He heard her question, but couldn't respond. His mind was locked. He knew Margie, but that wasn't her. It couldn't be. The word *NO* just kept repeating in his mind. "Tell me?"

Davina glanced at him. "That was a trap back there."

"No."

"Yes. I'm afraid your girl wanted you to use this damnable, twisted technology with her."

"No."

"***Improve the world***! More like *screw up everything*!"

"No. She can't be on their side! I won't have it!"

"Honey, just because you say it don't make it true."

He shook his head. "She wouldn't do that! We busted Earth, Inc. together."

"I don't know what to tell you. She wasn't bound. She told you that the technology was not so bad."

Tears welled up in his eyes. "Yeah, and I screamed, *Destroy Reality*." Melvin's chest felt tight and he bent over under the strain. He clenched both hands and squeezed his chest. It had been years since he'd cried, but here he was, bent over like a baby. His gut was hollow and black. Margie had betrayed him. Every part of his body and soul ached. He suddenly realized what he was missing. He'd always been the person in control. He'd never let any kind of stress bother him and now, here he was, a simpering emotional idiot that had gotten lost in a critical moment. He involved himself with another flawed human being. More than that, he'd let himself get emotionally involved with Margie who, more than likely, was never the person that he thought she was. How could he have been so wrong? As he sat there crying like an idiot, he managed to whisper, "F-F-Forgive me."

"For what?"

He looked up at her with watered half-open eyes. "For being a fool."

"It happens, Pal. I should've saw it coming. All the signs were there. I was too concerned about helping you."

"Helping someone is always good. What I did was more blind, deaf, and stupid. I reduced myself to being worse than a moron. ... What's the definition of insanity? ...doing the same thing over and over again, but expecting different results... I knew better."

"You mean Margie?"

"You're damn right, Margie! It wasn't me that broke us up, it was her bleeding heart. Another day, another cause... Damn her anyway!"

"H..."

"She was all I wanted."

"H..."

"All I wanted was her back in my arms. It looks like that's a moot idea."

"You can still help us."

"What the hell are you talking about?"

Davina turned the sedan North. "I mean you can still help us."

Melvin wiped his face and shouted, "Are you CRAZY!!! I just lost my other half and you talk to me about carrying on???"

"Margie didn't die. She, apparently, is working with them now."

"Why?"

"I don't know, but we'll find out in time I guess. I just knew I had to kill those guys and get out."

"THEY'RE DEAD?!?!?!"

"I had to."

He grabbed at the steering wheel. "We've got to go back and get her."

Davina pushed with one hand. "Don't worry. I'm sure she has lots of help by now."

Tears rolled down his face, but he didn't care, this was about his heart. He must save his heart. "We have to rescue her from herself!"

44

Davina stomped on the brake and the sedan's tires squalled bringing them to a lurching stop. Melvin looked behind them in fear of causing a wreck. Had she gone crazy?!?!?!

She grabbed her seat, turned, and with an outstretched arm, she leaned over. With glaring eyes, she screeched, "Look at me!!! Look deep in my eyes!!!"""

Melvin sniffed. He felt waves of strength coming from her. She was upset, worried, and probably a dozen other things. Being shouted at wasn't something he wouldn't normally permit, but she'd helped him this far, so he decided to listen first before judging.

"I DON'T CARE WHAT YOU WANT! Margie's been compromised for whatever reason, but you better get it through your head that she's a danger to all of us right now. Stop your sniveling and grow some balls! *You want to go back.... and die*??? We need you, man!"

Melvin swallowed hard. He felt sure that she could hear what rang in his ears. He hated to admit it, butt she was right and he loathed the idea of not being right, but this time, he was emotional and wrong. He nodded. "Drive on."

Davina resumed her driving position and accelerated. "I'm sorry I had to put it that way, but we don't have time to deal with uncertainty, especially not when we're fixing to be trapped."

Melvin lowered his head. "I've said this rarely in my life, but I'm sorry too. I was going to rescue Margie and go home and probably re-marry her."

"You mean you were married once before? What happened?"

"We both made mistakes."

When she glanced at him, he could see scrutiny in her eyes, a sense of *I can't believe the stupidity*. She turned back to the road, looked in the rearview mirror and said, "It didn't work out for a reason. Whatever the faults were, those things usually don't change."

"I know, but from what we went through taking down the other lab, I thought we had rekindled a different kind of love."

"Apparently, she's been bought out or convinced to fight for their cause. Regardless, she can't be trusted right now. I left her alive because of your feelings."

"Thanks..." Melvin said, his voice downturning. He wasn't sure he meant what he said knowing he'd see her again, but saying *thanks* was the right thing to do. "And, you're right, it would be far too dangerous to contact her again..." Feeling his chest ripple with cold streaks, he put one hand to his tear-filled eyes, slumped, then tilted his head back moaning. "God, help me. My heart tells me one thing and my brain says another."

"Get off it man. We have desperate work to do."

A deep anger ignited within him. How much can a person deal with and survive. His guts felt like he'd swallowed kerosene and her demands were lighting a match to his soul. "Hey! ... I've just lost my heart! Give me more of a chance to process this crap," Melvin said.

"You have until the time that we meet up with Rob and Charles again."

"Is that your plan???" By her scrunched eyes and down-turned lips that looked set in cement, he was assuming her answer was easy.

"Why YES! That was the whole plan. Now just sit back and get a grip."

"But why him???"

"Do you know anyone else that we can trust?"

"Well, I thought I could trust Margie. What if Rob and Charles could be..."

Davina put her hand up. "Listen here, Bub! I've been in Rob's skin almost. We've eaten things together that would you puke. We've taken lethal hits that would've killed anyone else and stitched one another up with whatever the hell we could find. Thanks to him, I have my cushy job so, when I say, *I know Rob*, it means I know his heart and mind because I've stitched up both."

As he looked at her firm body and her white-knuckled hand clutching the steering wheel like a vise, he thought it best not to bring Rob's loyalty into question anymore. "Sorry." After a long pause, he continued to ask, "And ... What about Charles?"

"You were there, same as me."

That was definitely true, but after Margie his trust was all gone. "I'm asking for your opinion. Do you trust him?"

"Look," she said with narrowed eyes focused on him. "I've dealt with him many times over the years and while he's playing on both sides right now, Rob says he's a good guy and that's good enough for me. He's been, *what I term as wishy-washy*, others call it political, a lot over the years, but he's okay. Is that good enough for you?"

From her perspective, Melvin supposed she was right. Nothing to see there, no reason to distrust... He knew his heart was breaking. It had been betrayed by trust and he was not going to let that happen again. "Yeah," he said in a quiet voice. He looked over at Davina and let his mind wander.

45

Melvin was silent from then on for most of the rest of trip back to D.C. He'd mumbled a few words when they boarded the plane, but even he couldn't remember what they were. His heart had been torn, for a second time, by the only woman that had ever gotten under his leather skin. He hated to admit his foolishness, but Margie had actually got into his heart once again. This rip wouldn't heal as easy as the last time. They'd not only re-kindled love, but established a working relationship.

It'd been a lie though. They'd both been lying to themselves and each other. How could she have been concealing a total lack of character? She had to have been like putty in their hands to change so completely. How could he have been so wrong about a person, not once, but twice? He scratched his head as is if his answers would magically pop in there. They didn't.

It was Tom that kept repeating to him that *people change* but *his wisdom* didn't include that sometimes it wasn't for the better. After a lifetime of being alone, he could use a friend now, not to tell him he was right, he already knew that, but to help him ease his heart. It was stabbing at him, teaching an old dog a lesson that he best not forget, *don't trust... live in the moments of life.* It was a lesson of the evils of humans, yet, Willie had *needs of the moment* and was telling him about it. Davina herself looked to be a very bed-worthy prospect on the plane, but he dismissed the idea quick. It might complicate things too much between them.

Now that they were back near D.C., he asked, "Okay, where do we find the wizards?"

She looked over, smiled, then back to the road. "First of all, this is not Oz. Second, if you want to *keep your head,* you'll keep it *down.* Lastly, when I get you safe, I'll call them."

"Isn't that a bit risky?"

"I'll bounce the call around the world which should give me about thirty seconds."

Melvin decided not to answer anything since, in her mind, there was no question, but if anyone had the ability to think of an impossible question, there was always someone trying to think of a way to answer it. They were dealing with government after all. An entity with unrestricted resources and no conscience about using them. Her words of caution weren't necessary. He knew that certain parties wanted him dead. *That was familiar territory.* Only now it was the big wigs instead of husbands, wives, and police for doing their jobs. Hell! His entire life had been pissing off people for one reason or the other by breathing or by doing the right or wrong thing.

Growing up in the orphanage was hard, but it was always his own conscience that told him right from wrong. He'd never even been close to being adopted because he was never personable like the other kids. He learned to despise his *goodness* but he could never break from it. Being a good person is who he was and he knew it, but it was not easy. Other kids were adopted easily because they gave that warm, fuzzy feeling to adults. He never could muster that attitude. It was lying about who he was.

As foolish as it seemed to others, love for his birth parents saturated his heart. They gave him life. Life was precious even a life such as Margie's. The pain from having her warm candle burning in his chest snuffed out was a terrible thing. His love for her hadn't faltered, but if her love for him had been what he thought it was, she wouldn't have been on their side at all. He'd been in love with an eggshell. When it was crushed and reshaped, the thing he'd loved was gone.

As the car came to a stop, Davina threw the gearshift into *Park*. Melvin did the same with his emotions. One life-road had ended. It was time to stop crying and get on with the business of life. His love for Margie would always be what it is. He couldn't change things. It would always hurt, but he couldn't allow his feelings for her stop him from pursuing what was just.

"Okay. Let's get out."

Melvin rose from his crouched position to see a wooded area with a lone cabin as the only structure in the immediate area. The closest building to it, within sight, was 150-yards away. When Melvin looked up from the shaded area, He could only see streaks of sunlight as they peaked through thirty-foot high pine trees.

"With this tree cover, we'll be virtually invisible to satellites."

Satellites? "WHOOAA THERE!!!! Being prepared is one thing, but this has gone crazy!!!"

Davina lurched towards him, grabbed his arm, and ushered him inside the door. "Geez, man! I've told you what kind of stuff we're dealing with! Get it through your head! Your life is over! My life is over! Rob's life is over! The best we can do now is survive and destroy this technology. C'mon, grow some balls!"

"Look! In the past four weeks I've gone through hell and back. I've lost everything that

I've everything cared about. I know you're right. I know I should shape up. I know what kind of people we're dealing with. I'm going to ask one thing though."

Davina walked through the front door, turned around, and said, "Yes???"

Melvin stared deep into her eyes of blue. Deep pools of life that were holding a lifetime of womanhood. He wondered how many secrets she held. They were made of stone and, in his hesitation, they softened. She started opening her mouth, as if to say something, but he moved an open hand close to her lips and shook his head. "Just give me one night of relaxation."

"*Alright*," she said in a rush of air, then put her hands on his arms and rubbed with a wink of her right eye. "I could use some rest as well."

Was she coming on to him? By the time she took her hands away, he felt Willie tingling again. His guts in a knot because his world was crashing and here Willie was craving sex. It was crazy! No, he wasn't going to give in. It was a terrible idea! "Where are we anyway?"

"Virginia ... I have hideouts everywhere. Like I say, *I have backups for my backups*."

"Just like Rob, huh? Always prepared."

"Yup, and on that note, let me give you

something." She rose to her feet and went into the kitchenette. When she returned, she had a clear plastic bag with a sort of white box--shaped device inside. "This is a beeper and it's linked to the watch I wear."

"What for?"

"Just shut up and listen," she said in a firm voice. "If this should go off, grab your ass and run to the bedroom closet. It has a shag-carpeted floor and the carpet fibers are much longer along the back wall. Grab those fibers and pull. It will reveal a hinged panel. Beneath the panel is a tunnel, but there is no light. Climb down the stairs and pull the drape. Be damn sure that you replace the closet floor."

"This seems unnecessary."

"You think so, huh? I've had to use it on occasion. The room has a light in the center with a pull chain. The small room is cool, but there are blankets, food, makeshift toilet, and a first aid kit."

"That much trouble huh?"

"Definitely!"

"I hope you won't need the room."

"Me too."

46

Davina slept on the sofa instead of sharing the bed like Melvin wanted knowing that she'd be up way earlier than he was. In fact, she knew that this hideout was about as secure as swiss cheese. Still, it would be safe as long as someone didn't look too well, but she knew that she had to go out in the morning and wouldn't be there to protect Melvin should something go horribly wrong.

Learning from the best had its advantages. That was Rob. He'd been around the world and back again in horrible situations. Over the years he'd recounted many stories. Through it all though he'd stressed many times to be prepared for anything. *Danger lurks around every corner, and you never know when or where it was going to bite you in the butt.* Each time he said it, his caution was proven to be wise.

She slept the night but only in short spurts. She couldn't help thinking about the danger that was all around them. Her sleep time was tormented by endless thoughts about ways they could be caught and what gruesome torture and death methods that would befall them if they failed to cure this insanity.

The familiar sound of her watch chiming

interrupted her thoughts. It was 4 A.M. and she welcomed the relief from her experienced imagination. "Time to get moving."

Getting herself ready took few minutes, then she dialed Rob and arranged to meet at Ru's Diner. It was the nearby slop-coffee house, infrequently busy, but open 24 hours a day. It was out in the middle of nowhere, but alongside Eastex Highway which was well traveled.

When she walked in, the place was near empty except for two scraggly truck drivers from the 18-wheelers outside. She immediately saw Rob and Charles sitting at a back table next to the bathroom and took a seat with them.

After being cordial, Davina asked Rob, "I thought the meeting was to be just the two of us?"

"I was meeting with Charles anyway and he wanted to tag along."

"I don't like surprises."

Charles raised his hand, "Let's get on with why we're meeting. Namely, Melvin Travis...."

"No worries," said Davina. "I just need to know what to do."

Rob raised a hand and said, "You two talk a minute. I need to take two steps and borrow the restroom."

"Go ahead, friend," said Charles.

Davina eyed Charles as the heavy-set man watched Rob enter the door. It seemed his interest was beyond mere a following of the eyes. Why would he be watching with such a keen interest?

When he disappeared, Charles turned to her and mouthed something that she couldn't make out. "What," she asked silently.

Charles did it a second time and with the sound of a door opening and scurrying footsteps in her ears, she realized with horror that he was saying, *Sorry*. Trouble was on the way. Davina put both hands underneath the table and twisted the facing on her watch.

Men in black suits rushed to their side. Glock 19's were in their hands and one of them said, "Hands in the air."

Oh, no. Here we go.

47

Without knowing who it was that had caught them, a hooded Davina tried to memorize distance, noise, turns and everything else about the trip to wherever it was that they were going. It was not too long before they had come to a stop, down an elevator, and into a room where their hoods were removed. "*Oh shit*, Charles, I know where we are."

"*Crap*! Me too! These green rippled, concrete walls could only mean one place."

"And I'll bet anything that it's FBI hiding behind that glass."

Charles gazed into the mirror. "Wonder why they caught us, much less brought us here? We have nothing to hide."

Davina knew that statement was a leading question to her. Had she hid Melvin someplace? "No, nothing." She was pretty sure of her answer or at least she was confident that her signal got through. What did worry her was a headstrong person like *her project* not obeying his orders, but knowing she'd done her best was good enough for her. She had no idea why the guy was so important, but Rob's orders were good enough for her.

The door swung open and two black-suited men walked in. Davina could see two more agents waiting outside the doorway. All of them were holding pistols.

"Ms. Davina Meyers, no talking, just come with us."

Wanting to say something and actually doing it were two different things and she knew better than even turning, but she did. She turned to face Charles behind her and winked.

One of the guards jerked her arm toward the door and bellowed, "No stalling!"

They put her in a room much the same as she was previously fifty-feet down the hall and left the door open with two men, guns pulled but not aimed at her, guarding the door. One of the guards said, "Have a seat at the table."

Davina sat in one of the chairs. She waited in silence and heard no noise from the corridor until the clacking sound of fast-paced footsteps pierced the air. The sounds became more distinct and louder until Alva Thornburg appeared at the door. The guards parted ways to let her in.

"Leave us and close the door," Alva said looking back toward the door. After it clicked, she sat in the only other chair and faced Davina. "I disabled the monitoring before coming in. Now, tell me, why in the hell were you found meeting Maywear and a washed up hack like Robert Milgrew??? And this better be good..."

Oh no! Davina could tell Alva was upset and she could guess that this VP knew what little was said between them, so she had to fall back to a cover story. "Well, Ms. Vice President, we met to discuss Melvin. It's no secret that he is headstrong and, well, he's went off on his own. I don't know if he's gone into hiding or what. We were meeting in an effort to try to locate him."

Alva eyed her with a hand on her chin. "Why was Milgrew there?"

"Rob and I worked together for many years both in combat and investigating as you know. I value his input so I brought him in. I also knew he worked on a previous case with Mr. Travis. I hope that was okay?"

Alva just sat there a moment, then said, "Is that all you have to tell me?"

"That's the truth."

"Alright, you know, we didn't find Mr. Milgrew?"

Davina hoped that they wouldn't, but couldn't see how they missed him. "I thought that bathroom would have no exits?"

"The report that I got on it says it doesn't have any external or internal doors." Alva nodded. "Well, Rob Milgrew was actually invited by Charles. He was leading a revolt against me using time reversion. The dual invite must've clued him in that it was a trap. I just don't see how he evaded us."

Davina blew a wisp of air. " I don't either and I'm sorry if I did wrong."

"You didn't know. It's okay, but if you think you can could contact him again?"

She shook her head. "Rob's too smart for that. His phone is probably at the bottom of a river by now."

"Okay. " Alva rose from her seat and opened the door.

"How about the cuffs," Davina asked.

"If your story matches with Charles's..." The door closed again.

48

Davina figured she had waited about an hour. She had no way of being certain, they removed all possessions, but she thought she was pretty accurate. That meant Alva was taking her sweet time and she could only guess why. Charles had accepted her idea of the cover story over the phone so she knew that that wasn't a problem unless he was double-crossing her, if that was true, she was dead. After all, she knew the guy very little. She guessed that Rob seemed to be uncertain about his character too.

There was one thing she had no doubt of though. Alva *was not* a trusting person.

She was facing the mirror when she heard the door click and she turned to face whatever awaited her.

Alva walked in and said, "I'm sorry for making you wait so long. Mr. Maywear was reluctant to speak, but we've got it worked out now." She sat down. "Take those cuffs off and leave us," she told the guards and they did so. After seeing Davina rub her wrists and stretch, she continued. "He corroborated what you said in full. We still don't know how Rob managed to escape, but it doesn't matter. If you contact him again, use him to find Melvin and then kill the pesky son of a bitch. He's caused enough damn trouble for our whole organization."

"Yes Ma'am."

"That idiot may have destroyed the only chip that will ever exist that can protect against the use of this technology. The other labs haven't even come close in twenty-years. Whatever Tom Soren was, he was genius beyond compare, and the secret of his chip may have died with him forever.

"Don't let Mike Curry get on your tail. He's been snooping around far too much for my comfort."

"Why do you mean?"

"Well, he's been trying to locate Melvin and after losing him, he began researching the backgrounds of everyone including Mr. Maywear and mine. He's looking for clues because he thinks someone is hiding Mr. Travis. I do too, but I couldn't even guess who or why."

"Anyway, you can pick up your things from the clerk down the hall. I've gotta meet with Senate Leader Gerard or I'd walk with you more."

"I'm glad we cleared things."

"Me too," said Alva as she stood and rapped on the door. "Open up."

Davina stood and followed Alva outside the door.

49

When Davina picked up her things, she looked at it close and noticed the serial number on the SAT phone was different. She expected a tag, but didn't quite know what form it would take. "This is going to be a problem," she whispered hoping that a magical answer would pop into her brain. She called Charles, who had already been released, on the blasted thing thinking they had pulled the old switcheroo to him as well and arranged a meeting back at the diner.

She waited for him outside. When he arrived, she said, "Leave your phone, clean out your pockets, and leave everything outside."

"Why?"

She pressed a finger to her lips. "Just do it."

Charles re-opened his car door, laid everything on his person in the drivers seat and closed the door. He stared at Davina, but she as silent.

She was leery about sitting at the same table as usual and instead seated herself several tables away. Charles sat across from her, laid hands on the table, and said, "Now that we're through being interrogated, what's up?"

Before she could answer, the waitress came over. They both ordered coffee and told the woman to get lost until they waved.

Davina leaned half way across the table before speaking in a soft voice. "How close did you examine what was returned to you by the guard?"

"Not too close, why?"

"My SAT phone has a different serial number?"

"So?"

"I'm sure they bugged it. Yours too more than likely."

"I wouldn't know. I never memorized mine. I never thought I'd need to."

She leaned back. "I guess being a field agent for many years has made me a little paranoid, but, more often than not, it's being that way has saved my life many times over. ... Learning from the best has its advantages. I wanted to warn you."

"What are you going to do about it?"

"The same I always do: adapt. Until I do though, I can't go get Melvin. That's for sure. For you though, I'd recommend acquiring a new phone and ditching that one. Can you get me a clean phone without anyone knowing?"

"No problem. What about wire taps?

"That's easy to handle."

"Do you know what happened to Rob?"

She shrugged. "I haven't got a clue, but I'm sure he'll turn up."

"If what you say is true..."

"It is."

"Then we probably have our own satellite by now."

"If I'm right though, they're tracking the phones, not us. Regardless, a change of clothes and ditching stuff we normally carry with us would be wise in case of bugs."

Charles nodded. "Agreed. If Alva is in on this, it's likely that the president is too."

" I thought President O'Reilly was a good guy, but we can't afford to take a chance. Do you know anyone *we CAN trust*?? I mean for sure???"

"Mike. He knows about the technology and he's a straight up guy."

Davina took a sip of her coffee. "You mean FBI Mike? He was the one involved last time???"

"Yes, he was, but I told him to leave a few details out of his report. He was going to go against orders to try and help Melvin but it went sideways. I guarantee he's one of the good guys."

She nodded. "If you say so. ... Alva told me he's been asking a bunch of questions of everybody. It's really making her nervous." She nodded again. "Okay, let's talk to Mike."

"Okay, I'll call him, but I'd still like to know where Rob is."

"Not before getting us both new phones! Don't worry about Rob, he'll show up when it's safe for him."

"I never worry about that guy," Charles chuckled.

Davina laughed and stood up. "He'll show up when *HE* chooses. When its safe..."

When Rob's phone vibrated in his pocket, he figured it was another damn robocall from a telemarketer. This was his emergency phone that had never before used and the incoming number said it was from Spain. He pulled the phone out of his shirt pocket far enough to see the area code, 212. "Spain, New York." Weird, he thought, but out of curiosity, he answered.

"May I please speak to Robert Milgrew," the man asked in a low, vibratory voice.

"Who is this? And how did you get this number?"

"Mr. Milgrew, it's my job to know the unknowable. I understand you are acquainted with a Melvin John Travis?"

"Yeah, I had dealings with the man, but..."

"They were classified, yes, I know Mr. Milgrew."

"Who the hell are you, Mister?"

"My name's not important, who I work for is."

"Well, who do you work for?"

"I can't reveal their name."

"Well, I don't talk to people I don't

know." He moved his thumb over the *END* button.

"You win Mr. Milgrew. My name is David T. Cogley and I'm a locator with over 30 years in my business."

"You mean a P.I."

"No. I make my living locating people and things."

"And you're looking for Mr. Travis?"

"Quite right, Mr. Milgrew."

"You're out of luck, Bub, I haven't laid eyes on Mr. Travis in three or four weeks."

"Oh, come now Mr. Milgrew. Let's at least be honest. You had Mr. Travis in your bunker not more than a couple of days ago."

"Who are you mister??? *Nobody could know that???"*

"I've told you who I am and I will accept that as your admission of truth."

"Yeah, hell, why fight it."

"Now that we've cut through the deception, do you know where Mr. Travis is as of this moment?"

"Why?"

"My client has an important matter to discuss with him."

"Like???"

"It's not necessary for me to know what the matter is, Mr. Milgrew, just to locate. I do know and *CAN* tell you that it appears to be a legal matter."

"Well, that doesn't change my answer because I don't know where he is exactly."

"Do you have any idea?"

"He was in this area, but I think you know that, but as headstrong as that guy is, he could be anywhere in the world by now."

"I think it unlikely. If you talk to him, call me immediately. It is important that I speak with him. "

"Yes, Sir."

"Thank you and goodbye."

"Bye."

After clicking off his phone, Rob smiled and said, "That guy is great!"

51

"This is nowhere and it's just right," Davina muttered to herself as she parked her car in a thicket of pine trees. The area was just off the main road, but the foliage hid it just enough to assure privacy.

Charles was already there and began speaking immediately after she got out.

"Here ya go," said Charles handing her the silver blob.

Davina took hold of the thing, flipped it open, saw the screen, the numbered keys, and closed it again. "Thanks!"

"It may not look like much, but it works and your contacts are there. Best of all, it's untraceable and unhackable. Don't dare lose it!"

Charles seemed to think that this thing was gold. It was just a phone, but to be perfectly clear of her appreciation, she commented again. "Thank you!" *That's it Davina*, she thought, *stroke the ego*. With Rob out of the picture, at least for now, she needed Charles.

"Well, shall we call Mike?'

"First things first. I suggest that we smash these other phones and throw them in a river somewhere."

Davina twitched her body, bouncing her boobs in the process. He noticed, but she didn't care. She had to deal with priorities first. "What about our old phone numbers??? *Nobody will know how to contact us?*"

Charles put a hand up. "That's all taken care of. Your phone has two numbers attached to it, but all outgoing calls will be from the new number *unless you dial *9 first.*"

"Good."

"In either case, I'd advise keeping all calls under a minute."

"*But you said the phone was untraceable???*"

With a nod, Charles said, "Well, yeah, but give an expert enough time and they'll get you."

"Does that go for unhackable???"

"*No!* That part was true. In addition to the highest encryption, if the chips detect hacking, it'll re-route circuits, put up blocks, and if necessary, activate a small enough charge to obliterate all of the circuits." He clutched his phone in front of her. "There is no way to hack this!"

Was Charles trying to convince her or himself? Nothing was imperative in her experience. Nothing was unbreakable. Pride made people blind and questioning him would only serve to irritate so she decided not to question his faith. She would just exercise extreme caution. "That's good," she said. "Just be careful, okay?"

He gave her a thumbs-up. "Roger," he said, then started dialing his new phone.

"Too cocky," she whispered. *What about destroying their phones before calling?* Davina saw his rat-infested phone, grabbed it, and walked over to her appropriated car. She placed the buggy things, one by one, into the seam of the door and smacked them as hard as she could. Gathering up all the bits and pieces, she threw them in the watery ditch nearby. "Good riddance!" A cold breeze caused her to grab her arms and rub them. The cold didn't normally bother her, but she felt deep within her bones a relentless ache from the chill which seemed to go right through to her heart. She looked through her foggy breathe and hoped this macabre feeling wasn't a premonition.

"Okay, we have a meeting set," Charles shouted her way.

"When??? Where???"

"6 p.m. at our spot by the lake."

Davina looked at her trusty watch. "That gives me just enough time to take care of some things."

52

Melvin sat in the small room, if you could call it that, for hours. NINE HOURS to be exact... and it was ridiculous. Davina just left him in limbo and it was sickening. She was probably dealing with matters concerning him, but, hell, he could take care of himself. He knew it was Rob's orders for her to protect him, but, geez, he was tired of playing the pimple on everyone's butt.

He grumbled and started whispering. He had no idea what his mouth was saying, if anything, he just knew the longer he sat, the more tense he grew and the more he talked to himself. What was happening outside? His grumbling paused when he heard footsteps above him once again. It made his heart pound. He didn't want to die. This was not the rumbling romps of earlier, but soft thumps. And then there was a pause...

"Hello down there."

After recognizing the voice and seeing light beyond the curtain, he pulled it back and Melvin said, "Davina! I ought to kill you!"

"Look, Bub... If you only knew..."

As he climbed up and out of the hole in the ground, he could think of nothing more than pounding her. The long hours of contemplated questions were flooding his mind. She held her hand out for him to use as support, but he ignored it and grumbled. Once he was standing in the bedroom, he asked, *"Where have you been?"*

She sighed. "Well, we were ambushed."

"Where???"

"At a diner near here. I was meeting with Rob and Charles there to discuss what to do next."

Melvin cleared his throat. "The same Charles that you said Rob knew and said was okay?" When she glanced at the floor, he knew he had her thinking.

"*He did apologize* but we all stuck to our cover story so it's all okay."

Cover story? After pausing a moment to think, he said, "Seems reasonable to me, but I still doubt everything."

"Me too. We were interrogated in separate rooms, so I don't know for sure."

In an instant, his jaw dropped and he was sure his eyes looked like an owl's. "So you don't really know about either of them? Geez!"

Davina leaned forward with eyes of fire. "Look! This is the last time I'm gonna say this. I know Rob Milgrew! I know him like I know myself and you can stick any doubts you have about him up your dark asshole because that's just where they belong! You got that?!?!?!"

"And Charles?"

"..."

"That's what I thought. I don't trust that S.O.B."

She gazed at him for a few seconds. "I don't know. Regardless, for the moment, I have no choice."

He was going to ask her more questions, but as soon as he opened his mouth to speak, she continued.

"I came to move you to a more secure location and more comfortable place."

Melvin saw her pick up a silvery-looking trench coat from the floor and handed it to him. "What is that?"

"Never mind. Just slip it on."

Out of caution, he did as directed, but asked, "I gotta tell ya, I'm getting pretty fucking tired of playing these games. Why can't I go it alone anyway? I know how to handle myself!"

"Rob told me to look out for you, that's why. You oughta know what *DUTY* is?"

"Yeah," he said glancing down.

"Well, unless I receive orders not to, I'm going to continue whether you like it or not. Besides, this may soon be over. ... Plus, I've grown fond of you and would hate to see you go." She winked at him.

Melvin smiled. "Well, I ain't gonna spend much more time sitting on a thumb enema. That's not my style."

She smiled. "If you *really WANT to die,* I'm sure you can give me the slip. I hope you won't have to play the dodge game for much longer, but you never know."

"I do too," Melvin said. With slow lifting hands, he continued, "And I thank you for your help. I tend to feel indestructible once in a while.

She stared with a cocked head. "Once in a while?" She smiled.

53

After delivering Melvin to another one of her safe places, Davina arrived at the lake and saw the familiar alcove that she had used many times before. She paused a few moments looking at Charles sitting in his car trying to assess his mind. He had a contemplative look, but nothing else that she really could tell anything by. It was just like an intelligence operative to perfect a stone face. His phone being bugged probably meant that whoever it was didn't trust him either and the same was true for all of them. It also meant that the 3 years built up trust where Alva was concerned was probably gone.

When she opened her door and got out, he did too.

"Hello again, Stranger."

Charles waved at her. "Hello there. Mike is supposed to be here any minute."

"Does he know anything about what this meeting is about?'

"*God no! I'm not crazy!*"

"Good to know." He smiled, but she didn't. They both walked to the center of the area where a car was pulling in. Government plates. It had to be Mike. The car pulled alongside Davina's and stopped. Mike got out and said, "Okay, somebody please explain what in the hell we're doing out in the middle of nowhere?"

"Do you want to handle that, Charles?"

"Yeah, I guess I should. Follow me." Charles led Mike to the passenger side of his car and opened the door. "Have a seat, Friend."

"Why?"

"Trust me. You're going to want one." After Mike seated himself in the swiveled chair, Charles took a heavy breathe and then explained in long-handed detail what'd been going on for the past four weeks, leaving out Melvin's whereabouts, with very few questions or comments from Mike. "We only know that we can trust ourselves, but we're at a point where we need help. Right now, we don't even know where Rob is."

Mike sat in silence.

"Davina, do you have anything to add?"

"Not right now."

Mike looked at them both and said, "You realize, of course, that if I'm not on your side, I'd just lie and pretend I was?"

Davina said, "That's a risk we had to take."

"Well, relax," Mike said, "I'm on your

side. I was on Melvin's side once and it seems that I still am because the issue isn't resolved." He shook his head. "I knew something was off-kilter. I had my hands on some of Alan Rouge's investigation who took over Senator Gold's investigation after the disappearance of Trace Hooper, but the materials but they weren't adding up. God! A person could go crazy with this stuff!"

"Trace who," asked Davina.

"Trace Hooper," Mike said, "was the lead investigator into Senator Lucy gold. We figure Mr. Hooper found out something about Ms. Gold and she used one of the prototype time reversion guns on him. We only know about him through Mathew Craps testimony."

"Oh! Well, where is this Craps guy?"

"We have him tucked away. Don't worry about him."

Charles spoke up saying, "Enough about that. You investigation was not adding up? How?!?"

"Well, like in my search for Melvin, people would always clam-up at a certain point. I didn't know it was because of this time thing. I realized the untamed, destructive nature of it quick when Melvin explained it four weeks ago. You know most of what we've uncovered, but our research all stops short of the head person or group. ... The team and I can't even get names. ... By the way, where is Melvin? I mean you said you were protecting him..."

"Only Davina knows that," Charles said pointing at her, "and it's probably best if it stays that way."

"Just as long as he's okay. And where is this Rob that you mentioned?"

Davina raised her hand. "Rob Milgrew? We don't know. He's the best asset that we have and we simply haven't a clue as to where he is. He got out of a room with no exits just before we were ambushed. We don't know where he is just that he's hiding. Probably for the best..."

"Agreed, but if you three are handling the situation then why do you need me?"

Charles stepped forward and held his palms up. "That's the point isn't it? It's just us. We have no help and we already know that Ms. Thornburg wants us to lead her to Melvin."

Mike's eyes flared as he asked, "*The Vice President?*"

"Yes," Davina said with a nod. "And we don't know why, but she seems to be the leader or second in command. She's put trackers on us and probably will do so again. Without knowing someone who we can trust, we're stuck holding a deuce waiting on a face card."

"We can't tell anyone because of the risk of losing everything."

"Why do they want Mr. Travis anyway?"

Davina glanced at the gray dirt with sprigs of grass. She had no answers and was ashamed. She needed to be better than this. She waited for Charles who, instead of speaking, shoved her shoulder. Without looking up, she said, "He used to have the only chip that protected people from the time reversion."

"Used to?"

She glanced at Charles, then at Mike, "Yeah... It doesn't exist anymore and the guy that created it died."

"So why do the want Mr. Travis?"

"We don't know. I'm sure by now they know that the chip is destroyed so we don't know why they want him out of the picture. That's one reason why we need help."

"What's the other reason?"

Charles rolled his shoulders. "We need help. We need to know who we can trust starting with the President."

54

Davina saw Mike's jaw drop for an instant.

"Why the president," he asked.

Charles brown eyes narrowed. "We already know the VP is involved. In fact, she is the leader as far as we know. Normally, the VP and President work hand in hand... if one knows something, the other usually does too... Every movement of each is highly scrutinized. We need to know if President Draven is involved because, if he is, that's a giant problem and we can't trust anyone for sure. If he's not, we're still in deep doodoo, but potentially have an ally."

Mike looked up for a moment, took a breath, then at stared at Charles. "I see. You want me to stick my neck on the chopping block so you won't have to."

Davina shook her head and with narrowed eyes said, "That's what it looks like, but it's not like that. You've already met with the president. The only one of us that ever has is Rob and you and Rob's retired, we don't even where he is. Charles and I are probably blacklisted by the V.P. and it would raise eyebrows if we even tried whereas you..."

"Yeah, I get it..." Mike got up, turned away from Charles and Davina, and stared out toward the lake. "You're asking a lot. I'm literally putting my life on the line." His voice got low and Davina almost inaudibly heard, "My whole life." He stayed motionless for long moments. When he spun around, his gaze was steady and his jaws were bulging. "Alright, I'm in, but if this goes sour, I'd like to know that my family will be taken care of."

Charles said, "I know how you feel. We're doing this for all families... *Yours included.*"

Davina saw a sparkle in Mike's eyes for an instant, but it faded quickly. "Let's just pray that this works out well. What proof do you have to show him or anyone else that this is the God's honest truth?"

"I have something," Davina said in an instant. "We'll have to get a digital player that can play and record wirelessly though."

Mike scrunched his cheeks with squinted eyes and scrawled, "*What???*"

Davina looked at his confusion and said, "For this assignment, Rob and I knew that at some point we would need proof. Uncorroborated allegations against a high official would not stand a chance. After we learned that it was Alva and we were going to implant me, I had a subdermal recording device implanted in my arm. It got me past all their security checks."

"Good idea," Mike said pulling his cellphone from his pocket.

Davina pinched the base of her thumb and said, "The code to connect is FEAZ35HAP9-OL-7989-Z1."

"Connected."

"Now go to 245.9.89.106 and login with user 1379024, password 1$#905_AZ_DC-1994."

"*Geez! How do you remember all this?*"

"Repetition."

After several repetitious minutes, Mike finally said, "I'm in."

"Backup every conversation, every meeting. Now just, *Download All.*"

When Mike looked up, Charles looked at him with pointed finger and said, "You're now a marked man. Guard this information with your life."

Mike shrugged his shoulders. "I still don't know how I'm going to manage to get The President Of The United States alone in a meeting."

Charles gazed at Mike's arm. Mike's attention was all on Davina. She knew he was looking for answers, but she had no advice to give. She'd been given orders for years, some she liked, some she didn't. The end result of all orders was always the same to *get the job done.* The ones giving the orders never cared how it was done or the concerns of underlings with questions. *Just get it done.* She saw Charles squeeze then wiggle Mike's arm.

Mike broke his piercing gaze with Davina and locked eyes with Charles who said, "There's always a way. Be creative."

Mike stared at Charles a moment as if in disbelief at how a career intelligence man like Charles Maywear could be so simple minded as to understate anything. All three of them knew it was not going to be easy to get the President of the United States alone anywhere. There was such a thing as common sense to be considered.

While Mike pondered what he was going to do next, a glinting thought entered his mind of just ignoring the entire situation and hoping for the best. His answer came to him swiftly and sledgehammer hard: ARE YOU CRAZY? His goodly heart had spoke with such intensity that he shivered. It had always done so when stakes were high. Its rightness had been guiding his entire life. Church attendance was a family requirement in his youth. Maybe that's where his moral compass came from... in Bible speak it was *helping his fellow man, standing for what was right and* true... but regardless, his heart overruled his brain sometimes.

He knew that Melvin had gotten pulled in to an awful mess last time. It was the same now. His heart was telling him to help the guy again, but on a more profound scale. This time there were a lot of big boys involved in a power play. If the president wasn't involved, it was against him too. The world wasn't safe if the technology became operable by the most powerful country in the world.

"I'll get it done, I swear."

55

Mike left the meeting determined, but without a plan. He knew what he had to do, the goal was in mind, but the thought of spending the rest of his life in prison wasn't filling his head with great ideas. Going his own way wasn't a new thing though. In fact, he'd made a career out of it. Do a great thing that no one else had the courage to do, get a promotion. Go against the system, get a promotion. It was always be right when everything else was wrong... Rules didn't mean a lot if they were wrong.

His whole career was made of being in the wrong place at the right time and he knew it. Was it right or wrong to stake his future on his judgment, to take on the most powerful man in the world? Davina and Rob had proven there was a conspiracy afoot, but if he erred in how he approached President O'Reilly about this and he happened to be in on it, which was likely, a bullet could be in his future. However, in their meeting, Draven seemed sincere in his concern about the technology and while a gut feeling was not much to go on, his was right more often than not.

As his headlights shined on the driveway

to his two-story home, his gut ache forced him to throw the gearshift into reverse. He noticed oldest son, Mike Jr., peep out the door and start running toward him. He left the car in Drive with a foot on the brake and put the window down.

When Mike Jr. came up he was gasping for air and gulping air. With all the voice he could muster, he said, "Can I go to the junior-senior prom with Marie? Mom said I had a talk to you."

"*Son*," he grimaced, "*Marie's a junior* and you're only 13!"

"But, Dad, I really like her and this is such an opportunity!"

It hurt Mike to see those expressive teenage eyes look at him with such agonized excitement. He wished that he could show even half that deep-seeded, desperate, world-ending, emotion in his talk with the president. "*Can this wait a few days, Son?*"

The boy's eyes lit with controlled fire. "Not if I'm going to going to go to the store and get the right clothes."

Mike shrugged in doubt of his answer. "Tell your mother I said, yes, but for her to place whatever restrictions she wants." After the boys gleeful shouts, he added, "Tell your mom that I won't be coming home for a few nights because of work."

"Okay, Daddy." Mike Jr. said, his face blurred by his ear to ear smile.

"Be sure to tell her about my work, okay?"

"Yes, Sir."

As his son ran back to the door he left open, Mike drove away without understanding why he was doing so. He had only the comfort of a history of his gut instincts being correct. He loved his wife and two kids very much and dreaded their times apart. They brought much joy to his life, but the discovery of time reversion had impacted his life in a major way. The notion that he could be instrumental in the final dismantling of the disastrous forces that not only perpetuated its existence, but were attempting to further its use as a force to empower an iron rule over everyone was bizarre.

He was only a commoner. A nobody. He was law enforcement and an investigator. He certainly wasn't anyone important in the grand scheme of everything, yet here he was doing what he'd always done: fighting for truth, justice, and The American Way.

After getting a room at the Holiday Inn under the name *Baggett Reeves*, he spent a restless night with intermittent prayer.

*

By morning, he was feeling his concern for country and family in each muscle and joint in his body. As he raised up, he felt the pops of stress remind him of what his day was to be like. He was certain the many reminders weren't necessary as he felt them weigh on his mind.

Nonetheless, contending with pops, creaks, and general stress would be something that he would have to contend with for the near future. The oath he'd taken those long years ago was to support and defend the constitution above all. His family was included in that, but his first duty was to his country. Elsa knew that when they were married. She understood that meant he would have to desert her at times, but that it was for a greater good. Her understanding made it easier for him to cope with his pains as he readied for the day.

When he left his isolation, the brightness of the day blinded him. It was a chilled February morn with little to no wind that he was thankful for because it worked well into his plans. Now it was time to see. He dragged the phone from his pocket and dialed. "Charles, it's me. I'm ready to talk to the president? Let me fill him in." Saying the last part was for the benefit of whomever might be listening. "If it can be this morning, that would be great."

"I'll see what I can do. Hold on."

Mike heard rustling sounds, talking, then Charles said, "Mike, the secret service said the president has two meetings this morning, then a twenty-minute break before he travels to Britain to meet with prime minister Traner. Be outside the oval office at 9:30. He will meet you at 9:35."

"Roger."

56

Lucy Gold was walking back to the senate chambers for a vote on a wireless zone bill when Justin came up to her.

"Ms. Gold, we need to speak," the lad whispered.

Lucy curled her index finger and led the twosome to her office. She knew *need to speak* in that low-tone of his meant *Important*. Neither of them said anything until they were in her nearby office with a closed door. She turned toward the naive pup that she'd financed, her glistening rouge blending into her skin, and snarled, "WHAT *in the hell is the matter?????*"

"W...W...Well, Ma'am, my white house source says that Mike Curry is on his way to talk with President O'Reilly this morning at 9:30."

She shrugged. "I know. You don't need to know all the details, but I will tell you that I made myself a sweetheart deal a while back. Mike also went out of his way to meet with a few other people yesterday and I've taken steps to be sure he doesn't make any more meetings ever. I'm tired of things going sideways. From now on I'm not taking any chances. Nobody gets in my way!"

A wide-eyed Justin said, "Yes, Ma'am. I just thought you should know I'll go now."

As Justin turned, Lucy spotted paleness in the boy's face and raised her voice to ask, "Justin are you okay?"

The young man pivoted, hand to his abdomen, and looked into her eyes. "Yes, Ma'am, as always. My stomach is upset though." With that said, he exited the room.

*

He wasn't okay though. He was far from okay. Lucy Gold had done a lot of crooked things. A lot that he knew about and a lot he didn't, but could imagine. None of it included murder either by herself or proxy, but it sure sounded like she was blind with her lust for power this time. He couldn't go along with murder, no matter what she'd done for him. He may not have grown up in the best of circumstances but he knew right from wrong and murder was wrong.

She was paying for him and everything he had was because of her. With her resources, she could wipe him out easy, but he couldn't go along with murder.

Justin stood frozen with his back to the outside wall. He cradled his arms in one another and rubbed while his guts churned. So long he'd known Lucy... What a waste! Was it time to ditch everything he knew? If so, life would never be the same. He looked at the gold watch that Lucy had given him at his college graduation and then stared at the hand that ticked the seconds away. Every bounce of the thing seemed to be pounding at his head.

He hadn't thought these things made any sound at all, but the ticking was loud in his head right now. Was it only in his head? Nah, couldn't be. 8:32 a.m. was a terrible time to be conflicted because it seemed like his stomach wanted to do somersaults and hands to scratch his eyes out for what he was going to do. He knew what it was, he was trying to stall and make some sense out of the only just decision his sense of morality would let him think of.

He headed to the nearest door and openness, wherever he could find it. The walk seemed to take forever, but when he got there, he gulped the air. Pulling a phone from his pocket, his fingers started fumbling at the screen. He felt numb and, without thought, put his fingers to work. When he heard the ringing, he mumbled, "Whatever happens, this is right."

"Hello. This is Justin. I need to speak with Charles."

"He's out of the office at..."

"It's an emergency! His family..."

"Alright, Justin, I'm putting you through

to his cellphone."

After a brief hold, Charles answered.

"Ms. Gold is going to try to kill you Mike."

"If this is another one of your tricks, Justin..."

"No! It's true! Listen, I apologize for everything I've done before, but you've gotta listen to me now."

"Okay, okay. How do you know this?"

"I just had a conversation with Lucy and she wouldn't say how or where, but it was definitely a final solution."

"Okay, thanks, and Justin, I know Ms. Gold. You better head straight to my Pentagon office so we can protect you. I'll call Nancy and tell her you're coming."

"Will do."

"And Justin ... "

"Yes?"

"Thanks! I'm glad you wised up."

"I've seen many bad things, but I'm not having anything to do with killing again."

"Good. I'll see you in a bit."

As soon as they hung up, Charles called Nancy, then Mike to find out where he was and felt relief to know that he hadn't been held up yet. He told him to meet up with his agents in 10 minutes outside the portrait gallery and they

would escort, protect, and make certain he
would be safe for the meeting.

57

Mike went by the National Portrait Gallery. Out front, he gazed at its familiar tall pillars in front standing as a righteous testament of the historical items inside. The decor resembled most government buildings, especially in this town, and while the look was magnanimous, it was an all too familiar site for prestigious buildings in D.C.

There were two black cars parked in the center of the lot. He started to get out, and was rushed by four men in black suits insisting that he stay put. They inserted themselves into the vehicle, two in back and two in the front pushing him in the middle.

They said not a word, but amidst the moving sounds, Mike said, "Charles Maywear said you'd protect, not squash me."

The man behind the wheel said, "Sorry sir, but we need to drive up in your car to not arouse suspicion and curiosity."

Squeezed between two warm bodies might have been a teenagers dream, but certainly not Mike's. He'd be okay with it long enough to travel the few blocks to The White House, but no longer. Being between two sweaty men was uncomfortable but being butted up against each other in a small car was unnerving. They were invading his space! He couldn't see it being necessary, but as turbulent as things were, maybe a wise precaution. They went zigzagging through the back roads, every shift and turn prodding his psyche more, until finally pulling into 1600 Pennsylvania Avenue and that long driveway to the house. Outside the front door were four other men in black suits and Mike assumed those guys were there to meet him.

When they all stepped out of his light-blue Camaro, one of the guys at the door walked toward them saying, "We have orders to take Mr. Curry to the meeting."

Mike didn't move. His instructions didn't saying anything about being "met" at the door. The agent who was in the passenger seat stepped forward and with rigid posture said, "Our orders said the same thing and we were told not to relent for *ANY* reason."

The other agent raised his hand, brought his other arm up, wrist to mouth, and said, "Excuse me a moment." He stepped back ten steps and turned half-around. Mike sweated the next 30-seconds because he knew that there was a pending impasse while the agents shuffled him behind and between them like a sandwich.

"Okay, but let me give a warning to Mr. Travis," one of his guys said. The wall of flesh surrounding Mike parted slightly. Mike saw one of the other guys grab a gun from his back and fire a blue light directly at him. Before he could move, an agent imposed his body in front of the shot. For an instant, he glowed, then vanished. The three who were left guarding Mike pulled pistols and killed the others. When the gun that fired the light hit the floor, it vanished.

Mike scoured the faces of the agents that defended him figuring on having to try to answers questions that he couldn't begin to explain. Not that he didn't know what had happened, but he couldn't divulge what he knew because of security. They tried to erase him from history and that meant they were desperate. That meant danger. Did the villains know he knew the full story? There was no way to tell. Regardless, he was thankful for his guardians calmness and simply said, "Thanks for all that."

One man answered, "It's our job, Sir. Now, if you'll follow me?"

What about the agent that disappeared? Mike wondered about his family. Did he have kids that were wiped out of history? What changes had happened because of that man's death. Then it occurred to him, the others had no questions because maybe they didn't remember the man. But why did Matthew Craps remember Trace Hooper's death? This is why the technology had to eradicated!

The agent looked at him and without an answer to his question and decided to walk to the door and open it. He surveyed the insides, then ushered the three of them to the door while ordering one man to remain with the bodies. The agent led the way through the oval office to the corridor beyond.

"President O'Reilly will meet with you here," the agent said.

From a connecting door came the wavy-blonde Misty Karmel, a white house aide, saying, "You'll have about 15-minutes, then the president must board Marine One."

Mike had been counting on at least 25-minutes. The time constriction cost him any attempt at easing into the conversation. It also probably voided any pretense of privacy as well. It made his position precarious, yet not impossible. He already had one attempt on his life and he wasn't anxious to repeat the incident by opening up too soon. The incident at the door could've easily made him dead, or worse. No, the best option was to get this done, no matter how brutal he had to do it. It'd be chancy, if it were done wrong, but apparently he already had a target on his head.

Several secret service agents towed Draven O'reilly through the end of the hallway. Draven walked up to him and asked, "I hear you want to talk. I suppose they told you that I'm fixing to go overseas and have very little time?"

"Yes, Sir, they did, but if you'll give me some latitude, I'd like to talk away from everyone in the oval office."

Draven looked over at Misty and said, "We'll step in here, but 5-minutes before departure, come and get me. Okay?" He shook a low hand at her.

Wide-eyed, she nodded and said, "Yes, Sir."

The twosome proceeded a few steps to the oval office. Once inside, Mike decided to trust instinct and stab directly for the heart. He took a breathe. Here it was. He was going to be find death or an ally. "Mr. President, please keep a low voice, but the VP Alva Thornburg is behind the time reversion research."

Draven's tough-skinned face stretched to let his teeth bare. In a low-volume shrill he scrawled, "*Whaaaaat???*"

"Yes, Sir, and to prove it," he grabbed the phone from his pocket, "listen." He pressed play it next to Draven's left ear and the audio recount of Davina's evidence played in a low volume.

It took a few minutes to play through, after which, Mike returned the phone to his pocket. He gazed at Draven's contorted face with measured sympathy. The technology was hard enough to swallow, but the thought of being betrayed by your closest confidant could shake anyone.

"A few of us are fighting the proliferation of this weapon. In fact, when I arrived here they tried to wipe my life out."

"*HERE... at the White House???*"

"Yes, sir. I'm afraid so."

Misty Karmel opened the door. "We really need to go Mr. President."

Draven turned toward her and said, "I'll be with you in a minute, Misty, *but for right now Get Out* and Don't Come Back."

A wide-eyed, Misty scooted back into the corridor and closed the door.

Turning back toward Mike, Draven said, "You realize if I was on Alva's side, you'd have just signed your death certificate?"

It wasn't a pleasant thought and Mike sighed. "It's a thought that occurred to me, but *I had* to take a chance because without you it'd be very tough. Plus, I believe you to be an honorable man."

Draven shook his hand. "You're right! I'm on your side. What do you need from me?"

"Silence. Most of all, sir, we need major force to permanently end this."

"Don't go through normal channels, but instead meet face to face with Admiral George Wilks. Give him the phrase, *This is a code purple.*" He grabbed a card from a Resolute Desk drawer. "Here is his contact information. His secretary should know the phrase as well." He glanced downward with a pause, then said, "Mike, do you think I need to postpone this trip and be here for your group?"

Mike considered the fact that not only was the guy directing him, but also wanting to be there for support. It was a positive sign. It also meant he wanted to be involved and probably on their side.

He took the card with one hand and reached for a handshake with the other. "No, Mr. President, your presence after our meeting would only add to suspicions. You've given me a primary key to continue the fight."

Draven pulled him into his chest, leaned into Mike, and said in a hushed voice, "I want you to destroy all traces of this technology and whoever is involved. *Stop at nothing or no one! No matter what!* Keeping me informed with Alva involved is dangerous so don't feel the need to. I never liked that power-hungry woman anyway."

When Draven leaned back, Mike saw the stern hard eyes of a combat-tested pilot of his former years. The man knew the life and death stakes of what they were fighting and committed the team, if one could call them that, and himself to the eradication of a technology that could change their worlds into something unrecognizable.

Mike backed up a step and snapped a salute. Confidence in this president soared in his heart. The man was in the office for the right reasons and Mike respected that, before today, more than he ever thought possible. "Yes, Sir, Mr. President."

"Thank you for the talk. Now, I've got to go deal with Prime Minister Traner." He walked toward the door.

When Draven grabbed the door, Mike said, "Good luck!"

"Thanks, I'll need it," Draven said as he disappeared behind the door.

Mike looked around the room a moment admiring the furnishings and thinking about all the crises that had been dealt with here. This was one for the books that might be released a hundred years from now. Wonder what they'll put in the reports?

He turned and walked out of the office, the same three men in black were there. They asked him where to go next and he responded, "That's a really good question."

58

Although Mike respected what the security agents did on his behalf, and, knowing that they were sent by Charles, they were to be trusted, he still decided to ditch them for a while anyway. His trust only went so far. They could've been working for the other side also trying to discover Melvin's location. He and he alone had first-hand knowledge of everything that happened before and could possibly bring their unholy network to its knees.

He took George Wilks card from his pocket, looked at it, and jumped into his car. As his rear-end plopped into the drivers seat, a thought occurred to him like a police siren is heard by a crook the instant he robs someone. His black Camaro stood out like the swollen red nose of a street bum addicted to wine. *Yeah, right, you fool. Paint a bulls-eye on yourself.* The rag-top, two-seater hadn't ever been a practical car for a family man, but, damn, he loved the style. Still, it had to go. It wasn't conducive to traveling by stealth and, besides, probably everybody in town knew his car by sight. Although he hated the thought of getting rid of it, for life-sake, he knew had to.

He pulled into Harvey's Used Auto, not

for any reason other than it was the first car lot he saw. He looked down the rows trying to find something that screamed *nerd-mobile*. Everything he saw was BIG. Station wagons, 4x4's, caddy's, red one's, blue one's, green one's... About a dozen rows of big gas-guzzlers that screamed *I have more money than sense...* He was walking back to his car when he saw an oily-black-headed salesman walking towards him.

The guy pulled at his tweed coat like a knight testing his armor before going into battle only Mike assumed the guy was anything but noble. "Hey there, Friend. Can I help you find something?"

The relaxed drawl reminded Mike of a southern cop trying to sound superior even though most were only one step beyond a lawsuit for abuse of authority. He thought to most that it was just a job, a way to pay the bills, and a chance for them to bully with a badge. Then there was that rare breed, like him, that was in it to do the good deeds of law enforcement. There were other classes to be sure, but he thought this guy was out to bully and help himself. In the interest of playing *the game*, he said, "Honestly, Pal, I'm not sure you *CAN* help me."

The man swooned, hand to his forehead,

"Man, you're killing me! I've got to help you, otherwise I can't help myself." He continued forward to stand in front of Mike.

"No thanks, man."

'Come on... At least give me a chance."

He was persistent and Mike didn't know if it was that or something that tugged on his heart. The damn thing kept saying *give Slick Sam a chance*. Gut Intuition had got him through a lot of things so he asked, "Alright, Man, just what do you think I want?"

The guy rubbed his chin. In a scratchy drawl he went, "Well, you're wearing a nice suit, driving a nice Camaro, so I'd say you either you want a truck or you're shopping for your kid, in which case, you want either want a small car or a tank for protection."

Mike smiled. The guy would've been accurate under normal conditions. "You're pretty good! Unfortunately, I'm looking for a small car and you don't have any."

"I wouldn't say that. Come with me, Sir. I'm Pete, and you are?"

There was no way Mike wanted to give his correct name so he said, "Richard."

"Nice to meet you, Richard." He took a few more steps. "Nice weather we're having."

"Yeah, I guess, if you like cold and wet."

Pete smiled and waived an arm. "This is

the back lot where we keep our small and midsize vehicles."

Mike saw only a few cars that matched his prescription, waved at'em, and started turning toward his car thinking leverage was a wonderful thing.

"C'mon, Man, my boss is watching?"

Mike faced Peter again and told him, "Well, that Navy Ford Escort might do, but I doubt the price is right and I don't even know if it runs." He didn't even finish the sentence before he was being ushered toward and into the car.

"The model might be discontinued, but she runs like a Jaguar. I just so happen to have the keys in my pocket. Do you want to drive her?"

Mike liked the car, but knew you don't tell a salesman to bring keys out his pocket like that. "I don't think..."

"Look man. Just drive it a minute. Help me out with my boss."

This guy was using the standard book of tricks. It was a lame ploy but since he wanted the thing anyway, he waved in resignation and told the guy he would do it just to help out. After a moment of phony *Thank you's* in that sweet southern dialect, they were off. It wasn't long before Mike guessed all was right and parked in the lot again. The men went inside and settled on price. Then came the shrewd part.

"For my information, look up the blue book value of my Camero?"

After moments of pecking on the desktop computer, the guy told him.

Aha! "Since my car's value is well over the Escort's, how about we just trade?

"I..I..I don't know. I've never been asked that before. Let my talk to the boss. C'mon in."

Mike followed the guy into the trailer and sat down. After being cordial, he went into the back and out of Melvin's sight. When he returned, he said that the boss said no, but that he could do it for $1,000 and his Camero.

It wasn't a fair deal. His car was worth twice the Escort. Feeling a pain at his temple, he put a finger to his head and scratched. He felt matter buildup comie off on his finger, he pulled it down and looked at the dead mosquito on it. One of many blood suckers in the world, just like the damn leech in front of him. He felt a burst of adrenalin surge through his veins as a fit of anger made him blurt out, "Alright, you thief, it's a deal."

He needed the anonymity and, what's more, he'd earned it.

59

It was a fit of anger that made him make the deal and it pissed him off to be taken advantage of like that, but he did it anyway. It wasn't out of responsibility, have to, need, or anything else, but out of timing. It was a lesson he'd learned from his mother that, if you see what you want, get it while you can. He was curt with the sales guy after being swindled and when he was driving off, he shot the guy the bird. Silently, he mouthed, "Fuck you!" knowing that if he were to try and buy his prize auto back, he'd pay substantially more.

Mike paused at a red light long enough to get the address of the admiral. He'd been in the building before but it'd been a long time. After a bit of walking around, he found the office. A busty brunette sat at a desk in the 13' x 13' office. After talking with her and not getting much information, he told her that President Draven sent him. With wide eyes she picked up the phone and called the boss. It wasn't long after she hung up that a tall, dark-head navy man walked in.

The guy had silver, gold, and cloth decorations fastened all over his clothing. He walked over to Mike, stuck out a hand and said,

"Hello sir, I'm George Wilks."

Mike grabbed the hand and said, "Mike Curry, FBI, currently working with the NSA under Charles Maywear."

"Sounds like you're a special man. Please come into my office?"

Mike grabbed his wrist and squeezed. "Is there a SCIF nearby?"

Long-faced, George said, "That serious, huh?"

"Yeah, I'm afraid so. It's a code purple situation."

George's shoulders flinched and his lips stiffened. "Follow me. It's a bit of a walk." Looking over at his secretary, he said, "Maisy, I'll either be back later or not at all, I don't know."

"Yes, Sir."

Mike followed George out of the office and into the hall where the admiral's face now turned to stone. "Don't say anything more until we're in the SCIF," he said.

Mike said not a word, but nodded.

60

Thirty-minutes later after winding in and out of buildings, they arrived at the steel door to the SCIF. The admiral had a guard unlock the 4-inch thick door and in the two men went, after ditching all electronics and being scanned, not having said a single word between them since George's warning.

Mike had never been in a SCIF until now and the procedures set his nerves on edge as if someone was shooting electricity through his body. This level of danger was the highest he would probably ever dealt with. The room had modest furnishings, just a table, a few chairs, two phones, and a powered off computer terminal, keyboard, and mouse.

George smiled, looked at him, and said, "Have a seat."

"Thanks."

"Code purple comes straight from the president and indicates a threat to our republic that the president may or may not be able to deal with on his or her own. So, I need you to be very precise in your description of the situation and *EXACTLY* what your orders were."

"Well, hold on to your guts, the story has

a lot of details." He commenced to tell his orders, the words, the situation, and Draven's demeanor. He knew the vast amount of detail was probably much more than what the admiral needed, but he listened in earnest without saying a word. The 40'ish man, balding with a graying fringe, would occasionally grunt an *uh-huh, yes,* and with an occasional question, but nothing more. It made Mike feel worthy of Draven's trust and that he was talking with just the right person.

"*The vice-president???*"

"Yeah," Mike hushed with a shake of the head. "Unfortunately."

"We need to be *very, VERY,* careful."

"No kidding," Mike said.

"Since the two labs are connected, we'll need to take them out simultaneously, but when we do, the V.P. is going to know about our attack quick!"

"Well, I've got an idea that'll keep him occupied for a bit."

"What's your plan?"

Mike thought about the question. He started speaking, but he felt his gut churn as soon as voice squeaked. *Don't say another word,* it said. As many *high-ups* were involved in this thing, how was he to know that old admiral wasn't playing possum? They always were hard to spot in the woods because they clung to those dang tree branches so tight that looked like part of the trees. This old admiral could be like that. His gut liked the man and it had been more often than not, right, but in this extreme situation, he was not taking chances. Exposing himself like this in the planning stages was enough. He swallowed hard and stammered, "I... I'd rather keep that a secret for the time being."

The admiral's face turned to stone and his head tilted a bit. "Son, this is NOT the time to be uncertain about anything. The danger here is as big as it gets. Think about it! The President of the United States, the most powerful man in the world, has vested you with his full authority to handle this. *Failure is NOT an option*! We MUST succeed! *You and I are nothing*! The world needs us now. Army, Navy, be damned, THIS is the greatest power the president has so let's have it!"

The intensity of this man surprised Mike and further confirmed that he was talking to the right person. It was important for all plans to be out in the open, but being vested with such great authority also meant he had to take great care with it. When you play 5-card draw, you don't lay all your cards face-up. Everyone bets the strength of their hand until someone calls for a show of cards. Then, and only then, do you declare a winner. This was not the time for him to give away secrets. His gut was telling him that he must exercise cautious restraint. "Admiral Wilks, I deeply respect your opinion, but having this power means that I have to be an administrator. That means keeping some things hidden. Besides, you don't need the diversion right now. Suffice it to say, it'll work."

George Wilks glanced down at his hands. "That makes sense to me, but before I risk men's lives, I will need to have that answer."

"Fair enough." His answer was good, but did the admiral let something slip through his fingers? "Formalize your plans, then we'll meet again."

61

"Ready to eat," Davina asked.

Melvin could only stare at her. He was a man of action and he'd been bricked inside buildings doing the adult version of hide and seek for way too long. Davina was easy on the eyes and they got along well, but he'd rather be out doing instead of sitting any day. In fact, they got along almost too well. Several times they went from sitting close to petting to ... Melvin didn't want to even think about what could've happened. Either him or her broke it off with each saying that now wasn't the time. After the long silence, his frustration made him say, "In all honesty, I'd rather be catching bad guys."

She smiled. "I know. Waiting to hear from Mike is getting on my nerves too."

She handed him a plate as he entered the kitchenette. It was filled with a jumble of potatoes, chicken, beef, and assorted vegetables. Melvin cocked his head and he must've had weird look on his face because she told him that it wouldn't kill him with batting eyelashes. He mumbled ignoring the cutesy eyes. She had fed them both good enough thus far so he figured this brown concoction wasn't poison, just unappealing.

His first bite told him all he needed to know. He never liked the skunky taste of hash but it would fill his belly. He took his frustrations out at the meal by chopping every bite of with all the energy of a shark ripping their food. *They must be happy creatures,* he thought, *must be nice to be able to eat whatever bugs you.* Unfortunately, he had to rely on Davina far more than he liked, because she knew all the contacts. A loner made reliant. He sneered in disgust.

He had his last fork of the mess close to his mouth when her phone rang. It'd seemed like so long since they'd heard from anyone from outside the walls of the house. Davina said few words then laid the phone on the table. "Go ahead, Mike, we're both listening."

Melvin listened as Mike briefed them concerning his talk with the president and Admiral Wilks. "I'm not quite certain whether I trust the admiral, but the president does. That's for sure! It's up to you but since we don't have a whole hell of a lot of choice, if he proves forthright with his plans, I think we should trust him. The final decision is up to you."

Melvin saw Davina's eyebrows fly up and then eyed him. She wrung her hands, then heard Mike grunt. "We're still here, Mike. A thousand things are winding through my head right now."

"I understand."

After she paused again, she said, "I'm understanding that no formal plans have been made yet?"

"That's correct."

"Well, follow your gut, mind your procedures, and get back with me when everything's a go or not. The president entrusted you to make the decisions, not me. Whatever you say, we'll do. Until then, no one can know where we're at."

"Mike," Melvin shrieked, "The V.P. is the head of this thing, right?"

"That appears to be correct with the intel we have."

"I want to be there when that huzzy goes down."

"I'm sure that can be arranged, Melvin. Anything else?"

Melvin looked at Davina and smiled. The end was finally in sight. She shook her head in euphoria reminiscent of an after-sex glow. He wiped his brow and saw her return his smile with the crack of doubt that made his gut ache. That one look told him all he needed to know. There was no time to rejoice. A lot could still go wrong.

62

Being lost in your emotions might be a good thing for someone in the dreamy state of first love, but for someone being chased down to be murdered, it wasn't good. In fact, it was downright horrid. At any moment someone could find out where he was and come with an arsenal of ammo to kill them both. That, he couldn't permit. One, because of Tom's dragging him into this fine mess, he owed it to his old friend, and himself now, to wipe all of those assholes out. Two, if the powers that be ever perfected this mess it would mean a literal hell for everyone.

Across the table was Davina. She had sat still ever since the call had ended as if resigning herself to will of the Greek gods. Now, in the silence, she slumped. Her breasts, which were normally perky missiles calling to him for his touch, were drooped in resignation of impending doom.

Melvin felt her unsaid pain. His toes ached for her many footsteps. All his body resembled her spent strength on his behalf. His heart felt hers as if its beat were theirs together. Margie had made him feel hollow inside, now the hollow had been replaced by her. She whose eyes were like the pools of crystal clear water from a young world whose wonders were many and its love of the life that it held was wide.

His dreamy thoughts was broken by the shrill sound of Davina's phone. Its screen lit up with the word, *Unidentified*, on top a 10-digit number. She looked at with a blank stare, but then told Melvin sternly to be silent, then answered with speaker.

"Hello."

"Hello. Davina Meyers. My name is David T. Cogley. I am a locator of precious items and I understand from my research that you are familiar with Melvin John Travis, whom I've been hired to locate."

"Wait just a minute, Mister! I'm sure I don't know you and I don't even know this... umm... well, whoever it is."

"Come now, Ms. Meyers, it's my business to know things others don't. I'm not involved in the nefarious mess that you find yourself in."

"How do..."

"Like I said, Ms. Meyers, it's my business, but I must say that tracking down Mr. Travis is one of the toughest jobs I've had in a long time. Tracking down your SAT was next to impossible."

"Well, if you so much about me. Why are

we talking?"

"I already told. I know you have Melvin Travis, *shall we say stashed away*, and the people I work for need to talk to him."

"Who is *Your* people?"

"That's not important to you, Ms. Davina. I don't know what the subject matter is, it's not important to my job. What I *CAN* tell you is that my clients are not connected to the crisis you are dealing with right now."

"Fine, but I don't know this Travis guy."

"Ms. Meyers, that's hogwash and you know it! It took me forever to find you, but I know you're lying. I also know from satellite tracking that there's someone sitting with you, probably Mr. Travis himself. You probably walked in with him."

Melvin saw Davina's face pale. She stammered. "How..."

"Because it's my business to find things that are unfindable. Let's just say that are a lot of different satellites. I swear... I'm not connected with the troubles you are having now."

Davina waved at Melvin, saying, "You may as well say, *Hello*." Disgust was obvious in her eyes and downturned face.

"Hello," Melvin said in a hushed voice.

"Melvin Travis! At long last! You've been

one of my most difficult track-downs! Now that I've found you... Since I'm on speaker I have to tell you that this concerns a legal matter."

Melvin scratched his head. "Mr.," not remembering the name, grunted, "I don't know you and I CERTAINLY don't know anything about any legal matter so go ahead."

"Relax, Mr. Travis. I didn't mean to indicate anything wrong or unjust. You see, I don't really know anything about the matter. I am just a locator. I find stuff."

"So why are we talking???"

"That's the question indeed. Get pen and paper. As I said before, my job is to locate. That's part true. In your case and situation, it's also telling you how to contact that nice lady who hired me. When you do, I get paid."

"And if I don't?"

"Mr. Travis, I know you have pressing matters to deal with at present. Normally, I would give your contact information to my client, but... I feel that you're an honorable man. I trust you. This is a such a simple matter. I don't want to go down the road of compromising your situation and neither do you. Besides, by now you know that *I CAN find you.*"

Somehow, if Melvin hadn't heard

anything else, that last part rang true with an unsaid, *the next time will not be so nice.* "I understand. However much I do or don't want to resolve any issues is moot right now. You said that you know what I'm dealing with right now and..."

"Take your time... Take a week, take two, there's no rush, but resolve this for both our sakes."

It sounded reasonable. "You have my word that I'll follow-up on this as soon as I safely can." Davina had gathered pen and paper on the table in front of her so Melvin stood up. "Handle the rest of this, will ya?" As she wrote with her head down, she nodded. He walked to the window and stared beyond its rose-colored curtain picturing what was outside the dimly lit blind. Davina had said that both of their lives were over, but realized that things always change. The only question that remained to be seen is how much and what was next.

63

It was 1 o'clock the next day when Mike's phone rang. It was Admiral Wilks wanting to discuss the plans. President Draven had given Mike full authority to make any decision that he thought was necessary but his gut remained uncommitted about the aging admiral. The conversation lasted just long enough to arrange the time and place to meet and two hours later they were face to face.

Mike thought it rather unusual to be planning a take-down of an Earth-shattering conspiracy in the back, sealed, room of a restaurant, but also thought it would be strange anyplace except the war room of the pentagon or the oval office. The admiral presented his plan while Mike tried to evaluate, not only the plan, but his opinion of the man that devised it.

Military was not something had ever had the need to have experience with, but did understand strategy. The idea was relatively a simple one: jam all communications, attack both installations at once cutting off escape routes, go in, capture everyone. Simple in theory... There were lots of blueprints as to the how's, personnel, lines of communication, etc., but that was the plan.

Capture everyone was easy to plan, but in practice it'd be more likely to capture some, kill some. Since this damnable logic was a given, Mike wondered how many innocents would lose their lives. Would the scientists be killed or just the pee-on's? What would happen to the survivors? Since the technology was known to these scientists, would they keep them imprisoned forever?

The fallout once this ordeal was over could be nuclear, politically, economically, and socially. He knew it, but the admiral was military, he didn't care. They had trained him in tactics and to not know why to follow orders, just do as that superior says. They wanted Mike and others like him to know why and evaluate good orders from bad.

The un-evaluating soldier in front of Mike rattled off counted considerations for success minus technical details. Mike mulled over the plan with only asking a few questions. Admiral Wilks answered each with assured confidence of success. The maneuver was expected to take 20 to 30 minutes to complete.

It was time to put up or shut up. The V.P. had to remain occupied while the takeover was taking place and Mike was no nearer a decision to trust the old guy or not. He decided on saying, "It's all going to be revealed at the appropriate time."

Admiral Wilks eyes bulged, "My God, Man, this isn't sandlot football here! We need to be precise so that I know that we have enough time to pull this off. I won't endanger anyone unless I know we have at least a snowballs chance in hell."

There it was, Mike thought. His gut quivers stopped. Concern for all lives... That was the key. He leaned over and whispered. The older man simply nodded and said, "We can work with this. I don't envy you having to pull something like that. You may very well burn some bridges for good."

Mike agreed. Besides burning in hell for what he was about to do, it was the only diversion he had that would do what was required. He cleared his throat, perhaps of guilt. "So when do we do this?"

"*WHOA, PAL!!!!!* All we have right now is a plan! I still have to get two teams trained to implement this stuff."

"Okay, how soon?"

Hands on hips, George thought a moment, then said, "Maybe 24 hours. I'll call."

Mike nodded and said his adieus knowing what was to come would take some planning on his part.

64

The clip-clopping that everyone heard was familiar to everyone on capital hill. The heels that made the noises belonged to Senator Lucy Gold and she was on a mission to find her trusted aide, Justin Peters whom she had not heard from since yesterday afternoon.

She was trying to find because it was odd for him to be out of communication overnight. He lived at her house on the backside. He'd occasionally stay out all night, but it was rare. She didn't care what the reason was. Whether he was boozing all night or having orgies was no matter to her, though she'd have preferred sex hound to alcoholic. They were both destructive, but alchy's were more debilitating to themselves.

She waved to passerby's like she was best friend to all even though she was only bestie's to herself. She knew it and tried her best to pull the wool over everyone else's eyes. She considered herself a great actor just like everyone else in Washington. After all, here, most people had to everyone's asshole buddy. Not her though. She only had to buy them just like she'd been buying her elections. She'd been watching others do it for those many years. It was easy. The biggest question was why nobody closed the ten-thousand loopholes. She would've fought that movement, just like everyone else here.

She was about to go up the stairs to the senate chambers wondering if Justin was there getting the notes ready for her speech and questioning of an FBI agent when she saw Ms. Fairview. "Barbra, have you seen Justin?"

"Not today."

"Dang, I can't find that boy anywhere."

"Maybe he's in chambers?"

"That's what I'm hoping."

Lucy started up the stairs followed by Barbra. When she got there, she worked her way around to her place grumbling and complaining about her world, in general, every inch of the way. The aides behind her chair looked up in silence and escorted her to the seat in front of them.

Lucy sat down and immediately asked, "Where's Justin?"

A roundhouse of shrugs, don't knows, and mumbles ensued so Lucy leaned over and asked Senator Peterson. When he didn't know, one of his aides said, "The last I saw of him was yesterday afternoon."

"Where?"

"He was headed to the Pentagon. Only

reason I remember was he was as white as a sheet."

Lucy sprang from her chair. She was heading toward the exit when she heard an obvious question at her back.

"*You're leaving NOW?*"

She waved an arm behind her and left.

65

Mike had spent a lot of time thinking about what was to come and was concerned about a number of things. There was no one that he could really talk to, no one to go to for advice, and no one to confide in without risking his own life, he only had his gut instinct to rely on. In as much as the president was out of the country, he was alone and responsible for everything on this issue. One man with, what he hoped to be, good instincts against the most powerful back culture he'd ever faced. Oh, he had good associates like Davina and Charles, but he was the head guy in charge of planning everything. It was scary, but someone had to do it.

His main problem was distrust. Everything and everyone... At least a president had his cabinet to confide in. He had his two cohorts but that's it. It was disheartening and lonely but at least it was temporary. He supposed that's how all power was.

The one man he was meant to trust and supposedly was trustworthy, the admiral, still bothered him. Nothing had completely convinced him for some reason. He'd went back and forth, first, not trusting, then he did, then... He couldn't make up his mind. "There has to be a way to be certain," he muttered to himself. If only he could trust in these things, but he couldn't say he did with 100% certainty.

The only way he could was to have someone on the inside to tell him things were being done as promised. After all, he couldn't be in on both attacks and take down the VP at the same time.

As he gazed at the sun as it was dropping low in the hazy afternoon sky, he gripped his phone and dialed. After getting through the secretary and the cordialness, they agreed to meet. Since Mike was five minutes away already, they agreed to meet when he got there.

As he finished the trip, Mike thought about his wording. He wanted his spy's not to be looked on as such, but rather as assistants. There was no easy way to do that. After he parked, he dialed the phone again.

"Hello."

"Hey, Rob."

"I haven't seen you since the we were doing surveillance on Melvin's location a few days ... What's up?"

"Hang on while I get Judy on the line with us."

In a flash, they were all connected.

"Okay, you two, I need a couple of spies

to keep me posted. Ostensibly, you are looking for stuff that the teams you're with have no knowledge of and secrets of national security, but don't tell anyone why you're really there. When the teams have totally taken down the establishments, call me. If you see anyone taking and not destroying any equipment or anything, let me know. We're trying to dismantle this time reversion

for good."

Mike heard a duo of *yes, sir's*, *no problem*, and *will do's*, then continued. "I'm fixing to meet with the person coordinating all this and make arrangements. They are going to call you directly after this, but they will pass along the code *M1 Priority*. After that do you can make your own arrangements."

His two compatriots acknowledged his second oration much like the first. "We can all be hopeful that the next time we talk, the last of this mess will be dismantled for good."

After they all hung up, Mike went in to Admiral Wilks. They barely said anything until they were in the SCIF.

"Admiral, I'd like to place an observer in both of the squads you're sending in to seize these two places."

"Observers? You mean spies?!?!?"

"No. Let me rephrase myself. You might

say that they are locators. They'll be looking for all items related to this technology. Part of your mission will be the takeover of these places and, fundamentally speaking, destroying all equipment, paperwork, data, and electronics in a permanent, non-recoverable manner. Their job is to look for and make sure everything is destroyed even the stuff that your teams may not recognize as being related to this technology. There may be items that your teams may not see and thee are items that are top secret."

"First, it was only to take, now it's destroying evidence?"

"It's not evidence. It's a technology that's not from our planet and anyone that has a working knowledge of it is a traitor to our world and is a threat to our nation and to humanity."

"Do we kill them?"

"Yes. The guards and, more than likely, everyone else will try to kill you. Their orders are to protect the research with their lives."

"As the soldier I am, I obey orders as given, without question. As a thinking, feeling, human being, I'll say this order stinks."

Mike couldn't help but close his eyes and squinch his face. The admiral was right. "I try not to think about it, but I hate this too. Some of these people might have no knowledge about this technology at all. These are Americans for crying out loud! Most of them probably have families... I hate it!" He looked up at the old man nodding and realized how caught up in the moment he'd become and how much he despised this whole ordeal. After clearing his throat, he said, "We just can't take any chances with this."

After glancing down, the older man said, "Unfortunately, I agree. I just had to voice my feelings."

"I know. I feel the same way."

"Who are your lookouts and how do I contact them?"

Mike handed him a slip of paper. "Here are their names and contact numbers. They're expecting your call."

"Are they ready to go?"

"Yes, Sir."

"Then the attacks will begin at 10 a.m. tomorrow."

"We'll be ready. I just wish my next task was as easy as today."

"Hmmm..."

66

"Davina was still in bed when her phone rang. She groaned as a hand went to her eyes and rubbed away matter from the corners. She grabbed her phone and, after seeing 6:47 a.m. at the top, answered.

"Davina?"

"Yes..."

"Sorry. Your voice is a bit scratchy in the early morning."

She sat up and cleared her throat. "What's up, Mike?'

"You and your protectee need to be at the meeting room at 9:45 a.m."

"Are you crazy?!?!?! We're trying to hide, not get caught!!!"

"Nevertheless, it is *CRITICAL* that you do as I say!!! You will be safe. I promise."

"Listen, I know we got you to help, but..."

Mike heard grave concerns but he had to deliver them both. "Listen to me, *you NEED to do this!*"

"Mike, I know we asked you to talk to the big guy, but not to take the lead!"

"Well, it's gone way beyond that. The president himself put me in the lead. *HE wants it this way*! Is that good enough for you?!?" Mike only heard pure silence on the line. He was a good guy and she knew it, but would that be enough.

After long moments, she said, "Any guarantees?"

"Just my word."

"Okay. On the basis of the big man putting you in charge, we'll be there."

*

When he hung up, Mike again wrestled with his own doubts about doing what had to come. If it went sideways, there would be no second try and to think it all hinged on an admiral he wasn't sure he trusted. He knelt, laced his fingers, and said, "Lord, let this go right." He stayed there opening his heart for a few minutes, then decided what must come will be whatever. He could not change it or himself.

Rising up, he took his time dressing knowing the events of the morning were either celebratory acts of victory or the last moments of the dead. From there, he pranced to the hotel's cafeteria for their complimentary breakfast. It wasn't a meal for a hero of the country, but it was a good in-between hero and dead-man.

He ate slow and deservedly so. Each bite

of food was meticulously separated from the others and chewed slow as if it were the most precious thing costing $5,000 per bite. He would swirl his tongue around each morsel several times to be certain of getting all the flavor before swallowing. He owed this to himself. His wife and kids were ever-present in his mind with each bite growing more so as the plate cleared. Whatever happened this morning, he prayed for their happiness and safety.

*

Melvin heard Davina talking in the next room but whether it was to herself or on the phone he didn't know and didn't care. He didn't like being tied at the hip to her but needed the protection. This was getting to grate on his nerves.

He had to admit, that it was a hard thing for him to accept, but it was true and he hated it. That anger was beginning to course through his veins like molten lava. His volumous fire started in his chest and its tentacles spread quickly through every hidden crevice of his body causing the release of adrenaline. Like the rapids of Niagra, the surge was one he'd felt many times before, but his reliance on Davina made him realize the need to control himself. His brain wanted to enjoy the calm of a morning, the dawn of a new sense in himself *to do what he must.*

His eyelids popped open and he jumped out of bed saying, "Something's wrong!" The tensive feeling was unmistakable. Cold chills ran up his spine and his gut knotted. With a grunt he shuddered. He knew the sensation was more of a premonition of what will be more than anything but hoped it was a case of re-living bad memories. As he twisted to his bedside, he heard Davina knock on the open door and call to him.

"Yes."

"Straighten yourself up as best you can. We need to go someplace."

Melvin looked at his rumpled clothes and said, "After 2 days babe, this is as good as it gets. What's up?"

"We need to go where I went."

"He shook his head. "Listen! I've been around long enough to know purposeful evasion. What's wrong with this place?"

With sharpened eyes, Davina said, "It's under the White House and..."

"*ARE YOU CRAZY*?!?!?!"

She shook her head. "NO!!! *We need to do this*! Don't worry about WHY, *just do it*!"

"He could sense her concerns so he lowered his voice while asking, "Are you really sure about this? If not..."

"Melvin, sometimes you simply have to take things on faith."

After managing a long breathy, "Okay," he asked, "And who are you having faith in?"

She hung her head. "I'd rather not say."

"*But we need to do this???*"

Looking up, she said, "Yes."

"Then I trust you. Just give me a minute."

"Okay."

After she walked away, he started readying himself to face the unknown.

67

Melvin looked around the bleak room that Davina had described as a conference room and felt foreboding as if all was life itself was at an end. His gut churned like the vat of a factory manufacturing poisons to kill all of human kind for the well being of some evil beast that savored human souls. He didn't know if this feeling was a premonition or his pessimism distorting his outlook. So much bad had happened in recent weeks. Humanity what a detestable beast!

He looked to Davina who was looking at Mike. "I hope we're doing something here besides looking at each other."

Mike looked at him and said, "We are doing something, Melvin, just have patience."

"How much patience should we have? After all this time, I don't have..." The door opened. At the sight of the Vice President which he recognized from TV, he felt his jaw drop for an instant with thought of, *oh crap,* consuming his brain. Anger overwhelmed shock quickly. They'd all been betrayed by a devil in she's clothing. He turned to attack Mike wanting the man dead, but Davina who grabbed his collar and pulled him back.

Mike rushed towards the door, the guards separated letting him pass.

Davina yelled, "*You fucking traitor*!!!"

"It's almost time for you two to die," Alva said. "Before you do, we'll first have that thorn in my side, Charles Maywear join you. But... You won't be regressed out of existence though because you have been instrumental in getting me all the power. You see, I started out as just the money person. The real power in this grand scheme before your involvement was Reggie Van Heusen who was killed in the raid on Earth Inc."

Davina said, "I never heard of him."

"I have," Melvin snuffed out. "The traitor that walked out of here told me about him." He shouted into the dim hallway, "BUT THAT WAS ALL A SELF-SERVING PLOY, RIGHT, TRAITOR?!?!?!?!" He heard no sound, nor did he see Mike.

Alva simply stared and then chortled a bit. "What's the matter??? I'm afraid your *friend* has gotten wise. You see, he's made the moves to dismantle all of my opposition."

"You mean he's a turncoat!" Davina huffed. "I'm disgusted at all of you. You're nothing but evil! *Pure evil*!"

Alva stared at her a moment before saying, "Maybe so, My Dear, but I have everything."

"At the moment..."

Melvin raised a hand and interrupted her. "We may we be down, *but I'm NEVER out.*"

"My dear sir, as soon as I receive word that your puny rebellion has been put down and all that everyone involved is dead, your lives will be terminated." With a twist of the neck, she asked, "Let's sit, shall we?"

As she proceeded to do so, Melvin couldn't help but blurt out, "*You Bitch*, if I'm going to die anyway, I'd rather stand, but I can't help wondering why anyone would be slap-crazy enough to enough to screw around with anything that could go so disastrously wrong. *I mean, come on, Snake,* even you have got to know that this is something you cannot hope to control?"

As she sat, Alva began saying, "*My Dear Sir,* I know no such thing. No one knows if the outcomes of change will be good or bad. It's just like life. Some decisions are good, some bad, but they all have consequences. I figure I can maximize my power and *maybe* make the world a better place."

A stiffened Davina shouted, "*You're CRAZY*!!! THERE IS *NO WAY* TO EVEN GUESS AT THE LOSS OF EVEN ONE LIFE COULD MAKE!!! *I'm not educated in time theory, but I know that each life has unending consequences. Like if Einstein had never existed, Hitler may have conquered the world."*

"May. And if we could've wiped out Hitler, the entire world might be peacefully united."

"And it might've been destroyed."

"*And if... and if... and if...* We can play these games all day long. It's just going to get us to the same place."

"So..."

"So I still contend..."

"I DON'T CARE WHAT YOU CONTEND," Melvin shouted. "You can't just wipe out people's lives. It's just not right!"

"I can and I will!"

"Then you're an arrogant, asshole, prick! *You can't control this*! I'm not only looking out for my life, but *everybody's*!"

"Melvin, you ARE a prick and that's why I like you. With that said, I still have to kill you."

Melvin opened his fists. He was convinced now that this was very real and put hands on the table and said, "Well, fine, *You Huzzy*!!! I think you'll find this much more difficult than you imagine."

Davina took a few steps closer with a cold stare at Alva. "You idiot!!!!!"

"*WHAT*???"

"In my seclusion with Melvin, I've had the chance to do some research on you!"

Melvin stared at Davina wondering when she had time to do ANY research AND *How*? They had been together almost the entire time since the bunker.

"I know that you've gone through near all of your assets funding this research and that you're almost broke."

Alva stiffened. When she spoke, her voice was noticeably softer. "Funding two labs of high-tech research ain't cheap. It's drained my personal and business finances, yes, but there is always money to be had, you just have to look in the right places."

Melvin saw a determined look in Davina's eyes. It was the same look she'd given him at the river. She wasn't about to let up now.

"Who in the world would be crazy enough to get involved with this and has enough money to fund this?"

There was an awkward pause in the room. A wide-eyed Alva looked to be frozen between telling the truth and what lie she should or could tell that be acceptable. The twinkling in Davina's eyes told him she had the truth.

"Of couse! It's obvious! It's Senator Lucy Gold! She's been trying to get her hands on this technology for a long time."

Melvin recognized that name from before. He turned to Davina and asked, "Doesn't she just almost crap money?"

"*YEAH*!!! *That unscrupulous Bitch* owns half the country. *She IS the golden cow*!"

Alva stiffened, then clasped her arms together. "Yeah, yeah, she is. I tried to keep that arrogant hussy out, but needed her money. It doesn't matter anyway. You two will be dead in a few minute anyway."

"Unfortunately..."

68

From the hallway there was a loud bang and the guards at Alva's side moved in front of her, weapons pulled.

Melvin stiffened. He had been prepared for this war ever since that first night of Margie's kidnapping. Looking toward the door, he saw Mike, the traitor, put his head in the door. Grrrr... Staying silent was the wisest thing, but rage made him shout, "Well look who it is, *Traitor Mike*!"

Mike's gaze at Alva did not waver. "Sorry for the noise, but I brought you more guards.

"Why," Alva asked.

"Well, I received word from the secret service that your safety may be in danger."

Alva stood up. "Down here?"

"Yes, Ma'am."

She looked at her guards. "You two, follow me." She looked at Melvin and Davina. "Don't think that you're off the hook. When I get word that your pathetic resistance is killed and I get the *all clear* I will come back to see you killed."

"Don't rush, *Bitch*," Melvin said.

"*Oh, I won't*! I've got something special in mind for you, Melvin." She began walking toward the followed by her secret service agents.

After they were beyond the door, Melvin heard scuffling noises and voices. Alva shouted something and then more scuffling. After moments of staring at Davina, who seemed as puzzled as he was, Mike walked in the room and toward them. Rage filled Melvin once again. He was sure Mike had come to kill them, watch over them, or other nefarious thing, and it made him ask, "*What's going on, Traitor*?!?!?"

As he circled around behind them, he said, "First of all, I'm no traitor. Second, I've come to free you."

"*What???*" He watched Mike circle around him and heard the *ching* of metal and then felt his handcuffs drop.

"It's true. Third, we have dismantled everything. The labs are no more. The research materials will be totally destroyed by night including papers, computers, hard drives, and networks."

Davina stood asking, "Why did you turn us over then?"

"While the attacks on both labs was taking place, we had to keep the beloved V.P. Alva Thornburg busy because the labs were constantly in contact with each other and with her."

"So you had to keep her from doing anything."

"Or running," Davina said.

Mike continued, "Or starting the research somewhere else."

Mike nodded, "Correct."

"Couldn't you let us in on it," Melvin asked. "We could've played along."

Mike shook his head. "Couldn't take the chance. Your reactions had to be genuine. Ms. Thornburg is very, very smart! I just couldn't take the chance!"

"From being under cover, I understand," Davina said, "*Apparently*, when you met with the president a lot more happened?"

Mike waved his arm from side to side. "Yes, but I can't really tell you more than that. He helped me get this job done and that's it as far as you will ever know. We did lose two FBI men to time reversion guns, but since Charles and I are the only ones who remember them and all records of them were wiped out, we have no idea how that affected our timeline."

Who, Melvin thought, but he soon came to the conclusion that it didn't really matter. It was done with no way of re-living a life. "Hopefully, it didn't change much."

"Hopefully not," Mike iterated.

Davina glanced at Melvin, "What about

the people that kidnapped Melvin's Margie?"

Melvin groaned. "Oh yeah, her..."

"Well, we still don't know who they are..." he held out his hands, "where they are..." hands down, "or anything... but *we think* they're loosely associated."

"And Margie???"

"Oh! We're looking for her! But all of these are minor issues anyway. The technology has been destroyed anyway."

Melvin reached out a hand, which Mike grabbed. "Thanks a lot, Mike! If my protector here has no more questions, then I guess that's it."

"No. I have none."

Mike started towards the door. "Then follow me out."

Davina got behind Melvin who followed close behind Mike. They entered the brightly lit area devoid of others.

Melvin had a feeling of déjà vu and remembered talks with Rob about this same technology. Where was Rob, he wondered. Did anyone know??? He considered asking Mike as they walked up the stairs, but he decided that he'd rather not know. He knew that Rob would make a grand entry when he chose to.

69

When Melvin walked into the Holiday Inn the cool air smacked him in the face. The air smelled pure, as of freedom achieved. It felt good. The air of a long journey completed.

As he fell backwards on the bed, he let out a big sigh.

"Feel good," Davina asked.

He smiled. "Yeah, boy."

"Enjoy it. This is the end. You still could've saved money by staying at one of my places."

Melvin knew he didn't want to offend her, but the thought of another night in one of her tight rooms repulsed him. Being tired was bad enough, but he was also weary of running and staying at another of her felt too similar to what he'd already been through. "Those are *YOUR* places... and we don't need that high secrecy anymore. ... As for this being over... Somehow, I have my doubts."

"Why?"

He sat up and propped up himself up with his hands. "The knowledge is out there and too many people know about it. It's only a matter of time before someone tries to use it again."

"That's probably true, but God I hope not," she said, sighing. "I guess there's nothing we can do right now except wait for something else to happen."

"Unfortunately not." Glancing down, he said, "As for me, my life that was is gone. ... I'm not sure what to do from here."

"Well, I have an idea about that, but I want to get comfortable first."

"Go ahead," Melvin said. As he watched her grab some things and head towards the bathroom, he laid back. Closing his eyes, he felt the smooth, relaxing softness of the bed. As he lay there basking in the joy of a mission completed, he thought of Tom. His best and only friend from his youth would be proud of him. The team working with him had done a great job. Other than the chip, which everyone, by now, knew he had destroyed, he still didn't why he was of interest.

He tried to think for minutes before the serenity of the bed on his backside forced the closing of his eyes. He managed staying awake only a few minutes before falling asleep.

When he felt Davina rub against his front, he opened his eyes. She had a pink satin gown on, her makeup was fresh, and a smile was on her face. The aroma of a robust, flowered, perfume was around her. When her lips met his, he reciprocated. When their extended kiss was over, he rolled out from underneath her.

After he sat, she did too. "Look, we need to talk," he said.

"Look, I know I put you off before but I was protecting you."

He raised a hand. "It's not about that. Is this your idea, *me and you as a couple???*"

She sat up. "*A couple???* I don't know about that, but ever since I've researched your life, I've liked you, and from the time we met that turned to affection and it's just multiplied as time went on." He hesitated so she continued, "Look, I want this and I want you to go on assignments with me. I'm not sure where our personal relationship will go until we explore it. I do want your sexy bod though."

"Well, you are such a very sexy woman," he looked up and down and down her body, "and I would love to do this right now, but..."

"But..."

"But... I was just betrayed by the woman that I spent recent years loving and caring for who is now to dead to me. I thought I knew her and myself. You see, I have a lot of loose ends in my life. I don't even know why this Cogley fellow wants to see me. For all I know, someone could be suing me."

"I see."

"Until I'm more comfortable in my own skin, I don't want to slip into yours."

"That's fair enough."

"I do like you a lot though and when the time is right, watch out!"

A grinning Davina said, "I'll be waiting," and wiggled her pink covered rear on the bed and jiggled her boobs.

70

Melvin woke to a ringing phone on the table beside his bed. He sat up and picked up the receiver saying, "Hello."

"This is your 7:30 a.m. wake up call Mr. Travis."

"Thank you." He put the receiver back in place and started towards the bathroom as Davina came out looking as pretty as ever. He relieved himself, then prepared for the day.

When he exited, the clock on the table said 8:47 a.m. so he said his *good morning's* to Davina who had gone out and bought a paper while he was getting ready.

"You should read the headlines," she said pointing.

He saw the headlines, *V.P. And Billionaire Arrested, Charged With Treason.* "Nothing wrong with that."

"It's in the news though. That makes it political and I don't trust anything political."

"I don't trust anything, *PERIOD!*"

"True. I wonder how it hit the news so fast?"

He shrugged. "Dunno." He looked at clock, 9:05 a.m. "Time to call."

Grabbing Davina's cell phone, he found

Mr. Cogley's number and dialed.

"Office of Locator David T. Cogley, may I help you," a sweet, feminine voice said.

"Yes, this is Melvin Travis returning Mr. Cogley's call."

"Hold please."

"Mr. Travis, I see from the paper this morning that you've resolved your difficulties."

"Yes. I'm ready to get this whatever deal is."

"Good, and since you called back on the number I originally contacted you on, we won't have to deal with security procedures."

"Uh-huh. Good."

"Please contact Attorney Sally Olson at 999-555-1606 as soon as you can."

"As soon as we hang up I'll do that."

Melvin cordially ended the conversation. As soon as he hung up and started dialing.

"Attorney Sally Olson's office. This is Tina. May I help you?"

"Yes, Tina, David Cogley told me to contact your office."

A cheery Tina blurted, "*You're Mr. Travis!* We've been looking high and low for you. Just hold on a second."

The line went silent a moment then another woman said, "Is this Melvin Travis?"

"Yes Ma'am it is. Referred to you by

David Cogely."

"Due to the guidelines I must abide by, I can't tell you what this is regarding until we meet in person. Can we meet this afternoon?"

"Where are you located?"

Melvin repeated the address to Davina and asked her about getting there that afternoon. She nodded, they agreed, and soon they hung up.

*

Melvin felt more at peace than in weeks when he walked into the reception area for Attorney Sally Olson. The walls were white sheet rock with brownish waiting chairs. After checking in, he and Davina waited about 10 minutes before being called back.

When they both got to the door, the lady said, "I'm sorry Mr. Travis but I am only allowed to permit you."

Melvin bent over a bit and whistled slightly. "Geez, what is this thing anyway???" Davina walked back toward the waiting room.

As legal aide put a hand on the door, she said, "You'll have to speak with Ms. Olson."

After entering the door, they turned and walked down a wide hallway and after a short turn down another hallway they entered a large room with a black haired beauty behind a large desk looking at some papers.

"Thank you, Tina. Close the door on your way out." She turned to Melvin. "Mr. Travis, I am so glad to meet you."

He smiled. "It's nice to meet you too."

"Please, have a seat." She pointed to a green-ish padded chair in front of her desk. As he sat, she continued, "Before we can talk about why you're here, we have to sign some paperwork."

"Okay," Melvin said in wonderment.

She lifted a page and turned it to Melvin. "This testifies that it's just the two of us in this meeting." She pointed. "Sign here and date here."

After he did as instructed, he passed the paper back to her.

She handed another page to him. "This testifies that, to this point, we haven't told you what this meeting is about. She pointed. "Sign here and date here."

"Boy, that's for sure," he said as he did as instructed and passed the paper back to her.

She put the papers together and said, "I am the executor of Tom Soren's Will. I'm sorry for the secrecy and long-winded approach but Mr. Soren demanded it. He left me with some unusual items that he demanded be locked up.

We just took them out an hour before your appointment."

Melvin had questions, but found his mind fumbling for words to put his ideas into a coherent fashion so he just listened hoping everything would answered in time.

Sara opened a drawer and brought forth a square glass container with a computer chip on one side and a graduation ring on the other.

An audible gasp escaped him. Was this really what he thought?

Sara set the container on her desk and opened it. Then, she brought forth a sealed envelope and set it on the desk with his name handwritten on it. Melvin's eyes filled with tears. The hand that wrote this was Tom's!

His hands shook as he opened the sealed envelope. Inside was a handwritten note:

Hi old friend,

I'm dead, obviously. I
knew my running away
would kill me. Even if it
were not for my bad
health, everyone at the
lab knew that they were
giving us a chemical
that made getting away

a death sentence. I
knew I'd die sooner or
later that's why I had to
trust someone to carry
on and I knew I could
trust you.

I know I told you that I
only had one chip,
sorry. Here is another
one. I lied to protect
you and I knew you
would destroy the
original. I just could not
let my life's work go like
that. This is a duplicate
I made after I escaped.
Hold it in memory of
me as I know you
defeated the bad guys.

The ring... In my off-
time, I got an
engineering degree from
LSU. This is my class
ring, which I custom
designed myself. It's the
most important thing I
have. It is a priceless,

one of a kind, testament
to the abilities of man.

That's about it, Pal.
Love ya!

Your friend always,
Tom Soren

After he was done reading, Melvin could
only stare at the letter. Why would his best and
only friend do this to him? Why? The word
kept repeating in his head.

"Why what," Sally asked.

He raised his head in surprise. He hadn't
realized that he had spoken.

"You know, quite often, I find that with
wills like this they leave many more questions
than answers."

"Yes, I'm sure." Melvin spoke low and
slow, trying to think while he talked. He
wanted to destroy this chip like the other, but
what if kept running through his mind. *Fear the
unknown* came from the darkest corners of his
mind. "I'll tell you what..."

"Yes," Sally said.

"I'd like to leave this in your safe."

"You'll need to sign some forms and pay
a deposit?"

"Fine."

After they did what was required, Melvin walked back into the waiting room.

"What did they want," Davina asked as she stood up to join him at the door.

He didn't want anyone to know about the letter, Tom, or especially the chip. His gut quivered at the mere thought that someone else could be continuing the research, but he knew the knowledge was out there. Some one at some time would surely try to start again. He had to keep what he knew a secret. "Just a bunch of questions about Margie," he said holding the door open for Davina.

EPILOGUE

Near the rippled aluminum hanger of planes stood Migel Estevez watching the awaited Learjet pull into deboarding range. It was slowing its motion and after its engines were cut, it stopped.

Minutes later, the door opened and the stairs popped out. Migel watched his friend and benefactor step outside the door and gracefully down the stairs. When she got to the bottom, he couldn't resist walking up and taking her hand. "Welcome to our land, Ms. Gold."

"Are you all set up here," she asked.

"Almost, thanks to you. The building is all set up but there are some equipment items that haven't arrived yet and a few items are having to be built from the specs you sent."

"How soon?"

"We'll be ready to run in every area within 6 weeks. Some sections will up and going sooner."

"Excellent!"

"Your living quarters are not far from here."

Lucy thought a moment. "And security?"

"The military will stay on high alert."

"Let's go for a tour."

Miguel pointed an open hand away from the airstrip, saying, "Yes, Ma'am."

***

NOTE TO READER

I would like to personally thank you for reading "Inalienable Rights". I hope you enjoyed it as much as I enjoyed writing i. It's been hard, but all life is hard sometimes. Lord bless all of you and may you prosper.

I hope you enjoyed the book. If you did, I invite you to let others know by writing a review on Amazon and/or contacting me personally.

Sincerely,

Mark Wayne Allen

Mark Wayne Allen has been living as a quadriplegic since 1982. Through the years he has never given up and is today an active member of his community. He takes a great interest in young people, speaking to them about life's problems at every chance.

While he actively publishes new items, books have remained his focus. He and his wife, Kelley, have been happily married for 11 years in Merryville, La.

Many of his writings still remain unpublished, but he hopes to make them available one day.

Website: http://markwayneallen.com
Facebook: https://www.facebook.com/authormwa